# Uncle
# Yah Yah

## 21st Century
## Man of Wisdom

### By
### Al Dickens

I am Uncle Yah Yah and I have something to say to you. Whether the fools accept these small truths or not, I could care less. I must have my say.

Some of you will reject my words on first sight, without so much as a second glance. To you I say just one word: *Fool!* But to those of you who have the courage to at least sniff at my words before proclaiming that they stink, I offer you a little jewel of consummate wisdom.

It is to you courageous ones that I address these words. The weakhearted can't endure this fact-finding trip upon which we are about to embark.

The weakhearted are silly people, afraid of their own shadows. Whenever Challenge raises his shaggy head, the poor cowards tremble and take flight, unaware that discovery is the fruit of life; the fools dive headlong into the arms of the very death they think they are running from. Fear to learn new things is the worst kind of death.

But let us leave the weakhearted, chained to their fear and ignorance. We have no time to waste discussing fools; in fact, the wisdom of a wiseman can be measured according to the swiftness he displays in shunning the fools. So let's hurry into what matters. Read on.

*- Uncle Yah Yah*

# UNCLE YAH YAH

# 21st Century Man of Wisdom

## By
## Al Dickens

*The responsibility for the Theology expressed in this book is entirely that of the author Al Dickens.*

"Literature should not be suppressed merely because it offends the moral code of the censor."

Supreme Court Justice
William O. Douglass
Dissent, Roth VS. U.S. 354 & U.S. 476-(1957).

Published by:
Yah Yah & Company
P. O. Box 55133
Trenton, NJ 08638

ISBN 0-9759646-0-7

## ACKNOWLEDGEMENTS

I wish to thank James Washington, Rubin "Hurricane" Carter, Tommy Trantino, Frank Earl Andrews, Nathan "Booby" Herd, Light heavy weight contender James Scott, Melvin Van Peebles, Richard Widmark, and a host of others who inspired me to do this work.

- I truly thank you

## DEDICATION

To my father who used to say,
"Boy, you ain't got a lick of sense."
Thanks Pop, I needed that.

To my wife, Wahida Clark Dickens,
"I love you."

# FOREWORD

This is one of the most delightful and thought-provoking books I've ever read. I found it fascinating, entertaining, and very easy to read. Once I picked it up I couldn't put it down.

I've known Al Dickens for years, he is a close friend and a man I greatly respect for his sober and witty approach to life's everyday problems. Al has coauthored and edited three books: *How to Publish It Yourself Handbook* by Pushcart Press; *Voices from the Big House*, published by Pyramid Publications and *Over the Wall*, also by Pyramid.

I've read them all and made a contribution to Voices, but this book is the turning point for Al. This is his long sought after podium, his opportunity to tell it his way and you will find that he does just that with amusing insight.

The heart of this book is Uncle Yah Yah's manuscript, which is as Al explains it, the teachings of his spirit guide.

Al shows a style all his own as his Aesopian-like fables unfold with the clarity and mystique of an ancient story teller. His exhortation that you learn about your society, understand what religion is and to know thy self are presented as a gift and not the dogmatic "Thou Shalt, or Thou Shalt Not."

Al is a lover of people and animals, a fact that burst open in a rainbow of fables and anecdotes that sparkle with home-grown wisdom and insight, making the manuscript of *Uncle Yah Yah* a pleasant trip. You are carried through a unique blend of reality and illusion with the smoothness of a magic carpet ride. This is a learning experience you will not regret or forget.

*Uncle Yah Yah* is filled with common sense, but the importance of this book, I think, is that it gives another point of view. Its virtue lies in the fact that many of you will have to admit that you've never looked at the world from this angle before. It's timely and full of keys to turn the old rusty locks that bind and constrict us in our daily lives.

Come, let your mind travel through this crystal clear world with Uncle Yah Yah, and you will return from this voyage a richer person. I did.

- James Washington

UNCLE YAH YAH

21ST CENTURY MAN OF WISDOM

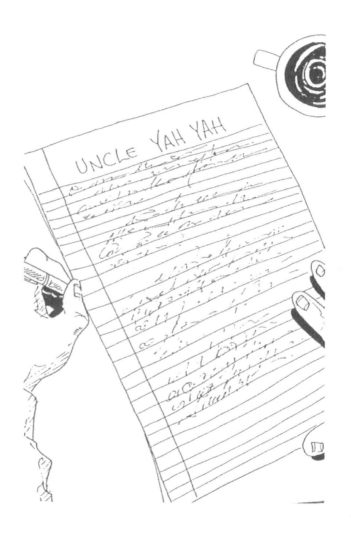

# CONTENTS

**Chapter One**

**DOTTIE**

**MY NAME IS RUDY HAWKINS, AND I'M A REPORTER** for the Essex Weekly News, one of the few black owned and black operated newspapers in the city of Newark, New Jersey. Dottie (Dorothy Schleifa), a beautiful black sister and typist in the office, was the first to inform me of the man called Uncle Yah Yah.

It was a Monday morning and the office was alive with the usual clang bang, hustle, and bustle noises of a press room. I was sitting at my desk putting the finishing touches on an article dealing with police corruption when I noticed it was almost time for the 10:00 a.m. coffee break. Just then Bill Diamonds, one of our best reporters, rushed into the office shouting:

"I got it, I got it!"

Some of the reporters gathered around him to hear the news.

"I've got an exclusive on that sixteen-year-old kid who raped those nine old ladies."

Bill had every right to be excited. He had been following that case for weeks. He threw his hands in the air in a gesture of victory and strutted with his chest out like a peacock. He spoke to the crowd in rapid fire of the details in the young man's confession.

"His aunt was his first victim, but she never reported it, and there are two others that he confessed to raping who also didn't report it," Bill explained.

"Why did he only rape women in their 50's and 60's?" someone in the crowd wanted to know.

"He told me that he was seduced by an old woman when he was fourteen, which was his first sexual experience, and since then he has only desired older women," Bill answered.

All this sex talk made me remember Dottie. It was time for me to renew my attempt at seducing her. I found Dottie at her desk sipping coffee and looking rather sober. So I decided to make some outlandish advances to humor her.

"What's happening Cup Cake? I've got a quarter. Heads you kiss me, tails I kiss you. What have you got, heads or tails?" I asked as I showed her the quarter in the palm of my hand.

"No thank you Rudy," was her curt reply.

"No thank you?" I asked as I repeated her words in a show of great disappointment. "Well, that's too bad for you Dottie. I was going to give you my Monday morning special, but you blew it."

"Why don't you give your wife the Monday morning special?"

"My wife doesn't know how to act when I give her the Monday morning special. She gets pregnant and stuff like that."

Dottie had to laugh in spite of herself. The ice was now broken and she began to tell me about her vacation. I had tried for one whole year to get Dottie to go on a date with me, but the closet I could get to her was the 10:00 a. m. Coffee break. Usually, she didn't talk much, but now, her first day back in the office, I was beginning to think she would never stop talking.

Dottie had spent a week at Paradise Gardens---a black resort---where she met a wise old man. Paradise Gardens is located in upstate New York, in a little place called Cuddibackville. The hills, the mountains, the forest, the rushing streams, and lakes filled with leaping trout, are pretty much the same today, in Cuddibackville as they were 100 years ago. Small wonder that it's a paradise for vacationers.

For 10 minutes I listened to Dottie describing the joy she found in Paradise Gardens, but the acme of her pleasure, she said, was when she met an old man called Uncle Yah Yah. She just couldn't tell me enough about this old guy.

Uncle Yah Yah, is not the Holy preacher type person most people think him to be. He's just like you and me, and he doesn't preach all that spooky stuff about sinners burning in hell after they die. There's nothing after death. If we don't get any heaven now, while we live, we just don't get any. God created heaven and hell. Both compliment each other. The angels are sent from heaven into hell and the sinner is sent from hell to heaven and when everyone understands the law, there will be no more good and evil and we'll have some peace for a change. You should hear some of the stories he told Rudy. They all have a parable and he uses animals as his characters. I'm sure you would've enjoyed listening to his stories. I felt so good sitting there listening to Uncle Yah , I didn't want to leave."

I had to interrupt her. Dottie was beginning to bore me, plus I was jealous because I could see that she was really impressed with this old man.

"Hey Dottie, what are you doing, writing a book on the guy or something?"

She gave me a hard look. No, it was more like a cold stare. I was beginning to feel sorry for my show of sarcasm. Just then her face lit up like a Christmas tree.

"Rudy! That's it. You're a genius. Why didn't I think of that? You've got to do it Rudy, please!"

"Dottie, wait a minute. I know that I'm a genius and all that, but will you please tell me what the hell you're talking about?"

"You said it Rudy. You said write a book on Uncle Yah Yah. Will you do it, please, for me? All you have to do is go to Paradise Gardens and interview him. Will you do it?"

At this point I had to slow down and take a better look at what was happening. This was the first time Dottie ever asked me for a favor --- just the chance I've been waiting for. If I played my hand right I'd have Dottie exactly where I wanted her.

"You really want me to do a story on this guy, don't you?"

"Yes I really do."

"Well I'll tell you what I'm going to do. I'll check it out with the boss and if it's O.K., then I'll do it on one condition."

"What are you up to?" She asked with a look of contempt.

"Don't get scared. I just want you to promise me a date if I get the story published. Now is that asking too much?"

"A date?" She asked indignantly.

"Come on Dottie, be reasonable. You spend hours every day trying to make yourself attractive and desirable. You wouldn't even leave the house if you weren't sure you were looking just right. Being a professional girl watcher, I am attracted to you. I really appreciate all that you've done to make yourself beautiful and I tell as much. Instead of you being flattered and saying it's good of me to notice, you are trying to condemn me. Where is the justice in that? Would you prefer a dude too dumb to notice or value your beauty? Who would look upon you as commonplace? Let's face it Dottie. You and I can see eye to eye. Think about it. All I'm asking you for girl is just one little ole date."

She thought about it for a few seconds and then said, "It's a deal. But not because of any of that garbage you're trying to feed me. It's because of Uncle Yah Yah."

Coffee break was over, Dottie went back to desk and I went to see the boss.

## Chapter Two

## CAROL AND JONATHAN

**MY BOSSESS, JONATHAN AND CAROL BARTEL,** are two of the nicest people in the world? They built this business from a store front, four page, monthly news letter, to a now, 46-page weekly, housed in a five story building.

Carol was in the office. I told her I wanted to do a story on Uncle Yah , at Paradise Gardens, New York.

"What! I don't believe it. You wait right here."

She rushed out of the office calling for her husband Jonathan. In a few minutes she was back, pulling her protesting husband by the arm.

"Tell him what you told me."

"I said that I wanted to write a story about Uncle Yah Yah

an old man ...."

"Oh we know who he is. This is a real coincidence, Carol and I were just talking about the possibility of sending you to Paradise Gardens a few hours ago."

"Yeah, I guess it is strange. But I'm beginning to feel like the biggest square in town, because it looks like everyone is aware of this old man but me."

"You've never met Uncle YahYah?" Carol asked.

"No, I just heard about him today. Dottie met him and she thought it would be a good idea to do a story on him."

"Well, you'd better not call him an old man when you meet," Carol said as she seated herself in the swivel chair behind the desk. Jonathan began to tell me what they knew about Uncle Yah Yah. I noticed the same kind of excitement in their faces that I saw in Dottie as they related their story. We talked for about an hour and agreed that I should go that weekend to Paradise Gardens.

I left the office and found Dottie waiting for me in the hall.

"Are you going?" She asked.

"Yeah, this weekend."

"Good, because I called Paradise Gardens and made reservations for you. It's all set."

"Oh yeah. Well why don't you come with me. You might as well start paying up?"

"The agreement was that I give you a date after

publication, not before. So I'll see you when you get back. Give Uncle Yah Yah my love."

"How about me? I can use a little love."

"I have to go now Rudy. I've got a lot of work to finish. I'll see you later." She started down the hall.

"Well can't I get a little kiss or a hug as a down payment or a show of good faith, or something like that?" I called out to her. But she just laughed and waved bye bye.

I went back to my desk and started writing the information I had collected so far. Uncle Yah Yah is a story teller. In conversation he would relate amusing anecdotes to prove his point. He has a different philosophy concerning God and the Devil, sin and righteousness. He claims that he teaches the Attainment of the Third Power, which he explains as a high state of consciousness that allows a person to use the creative force of good and evil to achieve the state of perfection. Perfection, he claims, is Godship. He first tried his hand a preaching in New York City in 1950, but was run out of the church for teaching what he called the "virtue of sin."

He then decides to move into the hills and mountains of Cuddibackville, New York. He lived in a log cabin and became known as the old man on the mountain. Soon people would go on hikes to see him. They would return telling the stories that Yah Yah had told them and his fame spread.

A black woman by the name of Sally Walters owned a large part of the land in that area. She is the one who built the resort. She realized the attraction of Uncle Yah Yah so to keep him there she built a beautiful ranch style home for him at the resort. He got married and began to live a normal life. His wife, Willie Mae, is much younger than he and they have four children.

The resort caters to a black clientele and is very successful. Black professional people are known to come from all parts of the country to consult with Uncle Yah Yah.

That was all the information I had, but my interest in the old man was greatly increased. A black man, famous for his wisdom and understanding, was a story that must be written. In the not too distant past, blackmen were noted for singing, dancing and running real fast, so this is good news.

## Chapter Three

## PARADISE GARDENS

**AS YOU PROBABLY ALREADY KNOW, NEW JERSEY** has some of the best super highways in the world. I couldn't find any argument with that fact July 13, 1973, Friday morning, as I cruised at fifty miles an hour down the parkway headed for Paradise Gardens. The Garden State was really living up to its reputation. The scenery was beautiful. I was completely relaxed. Listening to soft music and feeling very good, but then all hell broke loose.

Every year I trade-in my old Cadillac for a new one. It has been my experience that every time I take a trip I get stopped by the police unnecessarily. It seems that they every black man driving a new Cadillac is a dope pusher, a pimp, or a thief. I had begun to resent being stopped by these over zealous cops.

When my rear view mirror focused on the red blinking light of a state police car, my whole day

was crushed like a paper bag and tossed into the trash can.  Now what in the hell could this fool want?  I pulled over to the side of the road.

"May I see your driver's license and registration?"  Asked the six foot, John Wayne type trooper.

"What am I being stopped for?  Was I speeding or something?"  I asked, getting more excited by the second.

"Your driver's license and registration,' he persisted.

"I'm not going to show you nothing.  I know my rights.  I haven't done anything wrong and I don't have to take all this unnecessary provocation.  All you guys are just alike.  Every time you see a Blackman in a new car you pounce on him like some kind of animal.  I'm not going to stand for that...."

You can show me your driver's license and registration now, or you can show it to me at the station house.  The choice is yours mister."

\*      \*      \*

That sounded too much like a threat.  I realized I was beat so I gave him my identification bill-fold.  He looked at my press card and said,

"You are a reporter Mr. Hawkins?"

"Yeah, I'm a newsman."  I told him as I stared into his eyes.

"Alright you can go," he said as he gave back my billfold.

I drove back onto the road, but what had been a beautiful day for me was now ruined, because I was so hot I could've blown my top. That son of a bitch had no right to stop me. All those white cracker cops are the same I said to myself. I don't usually drink, but I needed one then. I decided to stop at the first place I could find.

The sign read TOP HAT BAR & GRILL and a smaller sign said Go Go Girls. I walked up to the bar and ordered a Scotch and soda. Still angry, I didn't even look the place over. I just wanted a drink. A black girl who looked like a teenager came and sat on the bar stool next to mine.

"My name is Elsie. Are you looking for a little fun?" Twenty five dollars and w can go to my room," she said smiling like the cat that just swallowed the mouse.

If it had been any other time I wouldn't have hesitated to take her up on that offer. She looked that good, but I was all messed up inside and I didn't want to be bothered. I looked at that poor girl as if I was about to spit in her face.

"Get the hell away from me, whore." She disappeared as silently as she had come. "Bartender, give me another of the same.

I had to get a grip on myself, but I didn't know what was really eating me. Yeah that cop had got on my nerves, but that was no cause for me to be as up-tight as I was. I felt much better by the time I was back in my care and on the road. Maybe it was the Scotch.

I arrived at Paradise Gardens at about 2:00 p.m. My first impression was that this is Paradise. If I said it's a beautiful place that would be only half the truth. I think that Paradise Gardens is the closest acreage to that place called heaven any of us could ever hope to see on this side of the grave. I saw people swimming in an Olympic size pool. Smiling faces picnicking on the spacious lawns. Party people dancing in the casino to the music of a live band. The tennis courts and miniature golf courses were alive with happy activity. Young and old dashed from one bungalow to the next, in search of a livelier party. People were everywhere. I learned later that July and August are the busiest months of the year.

After looking the place over a little, I went to the office. I walked in just in time to catch the last part of an argument between the receptionist and a party of seven people.

I stood at the side of the receptionist's desk to wait my turn and listen to what was going on. A fat woman dressed like a Muslim in a headpiece and long dress came in with a little boy about nine years old dressed in a blue suit and bow tie. The kid marched right up to the side of me and just stood there at attention.

"Well, why didn't you tell me on the phone that you were all filled up?"

"Mr. Johnson, this is the busiest time of the year for us and we just can't handle all the guests that make reservations. Some people make reservations and never show up. So we have to work it out by accepting the reservation, but on a first come first served basis. I know it's not fair to people like you, but what would you do if you were in our place? Listen, it might not be as bad as all that. There is a lodge about a mile down the road called White House Inn. They have vacancies. You could lodge there and use all the facilities here. Do you have a car?"

"Yes we have a car, but I still don't like being

tricked. We made reservations here, not a mile down the road. You say we can sleep at the White House Inn and we won't have to pay anything for using your facilities here?" Mr. Johnson asked.

"That's right. No charge. Just enjoy yourself. Oh, just one thing. If you have your meals here, you can pay by the day, which is $10.00 per person. Or, you can give me $140.00 for your party of seven. That will cover the four days you intend to be with us. Okay?"

"Alright, here's the money for the Johnson party. Now, what about that preacher Uncle Yah Yah. Do we have to pay to see him?"

"No, there's no charge to see Uncle Yah Yah. But he is not a preacher, in that, he doesn't have a church. He lives in that ranch style house just on the other side of the tennis courts. He is home most of the time, so you can go and see him whenever you like. Here's you receipt Mr. Johnson."

"Alright. But don't say we ain't got reservations when we come in to eat. You hear?"

"Okay Mr. Johnson. I won't. That I promise. Next please."

The telephone rang and the receptionist answered it. The woman with the little boy moved in front of me. The receptionist reached for the microphone.

"Paging Mrs. Sally Walters. Paging Mrs. Walters. Report to the office."

I moved away from the counter to wait for Mrs. Walters. I didn't have to wait long. Through a side door came Mrs. Walters wearing a chef's hat and a big white apron.   She was a big woman, brown skin, gray hair, was the prototype of what grandmothers all over the world look like.

Her voice was soft and had a pleasant ring to it.  When she hung up the phone, I went over to her and said, "Are you Mrs. Walters?"

"Yes, but just a minute sweetheart.  Sue, honey.  How many have you turned away?"

"Ah, let me see.  Fifteen so far."

"Are you sending them to the White House Inn?  Billy says they still have room in the annex for about twenty more."

"Yes.  I just sent a party of seven over there."

"Good girl.  Okay, but call me if you need any help out here."

"I'm fine.  Don't worry about me, I can handle it."

Mrs. Walters turned to me and said, "Yes, Sweetheart.  You wanted to see me about something?"

"I'm Rudy Hawkins," I said as I pulled out my press card as if it was a policeman's badge.  "I came here to write a story about Uncle Yah Yah.  I called a few days ago for a reservation this weekend."

"Oh, how nice Sweetheart.  I'm so glad you could come.  Yes, Sue. This is Mr. Hawkins from the newspaper.  Where did you place him?"

"He has a single cabin.  Number ten."

"Alright sweetheart. Mr. Hawkins, you have cabin ten, and please let me know if you need anything. I have to hurry now. I left my biscuits in the oven."

"Thank you Mrs. Walters. When will I get the chance to talk with you? I have some questions to ask?"

"Can you come back here tonight about 7:30?"

"Yes. I'll be here."

"Very good. I will see you then Mr. Hawkins", she said as she left the same way she came.

## Chapter Four

### FREDA

**I TOOK MY SUITCASE AND WENT TO CABIN TEN.** It wasn't all that modern, but it was very clean. I decided to freshen up and lie down to relax a little before I started the work I'd come here for. I had just finished brushing my teeth when someone knocked at the door.

"Yeah. It's open."

"Cleaning lady's here. Are you decent?"

"Come on in."

A woman walked into the room supported by the most beautiful pair of legs in the world. She looked to be in her early twenties, and she had a rich brown complexion. She was shapely enough to put a Coca Cola bottle to shame. Her teeth and the whites of her eyes were like pearls, and the dimples in her cheeks were as big as nickels.

She was carrying two sheets and a pillow case draped over her arm. I stood staring at her legs as she walked over to the bed and dropped the sheets. She turned and caught me in the act of lustfully feasting my eyes.

She smiled and said, "So you're going to write a story about Uncle Yah Yah, huh?"

"Yes. But I just got here, so how could you know that?"

"Sue, the receptionist, told me when she sent me over with the linen."

Oh, well the bed looks like it's made already," I said. She pulled away the bed spread, revealing a bare pillow and mattress then said, "We only use sheets when the cabin is occupied."

"What's your name?"

"Freda. And yours is Mr. Hawkins, right?"

"That's Rudy to you."

"O.K. Rudy." She said as she went about her business of making the bed. I stood there like a fool checking out her legs. You might say I have a leg fetish and you would be absolutely right. I should impress upon you that when I say that the woman had beautiful legs, that I know what I'm talking about. Hey, Freda's legs were out of sight."

"Rudy, do you like what you see?"

"Huh. What did you say?"

"It's alright Rudy. No need to be bashful. The commodity is marketable and has been for two years now. It all started here. I came here with some friends from college to work the summer. One night a doctor made an offer that I couldn't refuse -- a hundred dollars for fifteen minutes work. Since then the number of offers has escalated to an astronomical figure, but so has my bank account. And from the way that you're watching me, you might be contemplating a sizeable contribution, so let me assure you that what you purchase is guaranteed to satisfy."

"Freda, I really appreciate your frankness and any man in his right mind and body would leap at an opportunity to make a contribution to such a worthy cause, but I'm a poor man. I came here to work, and I can't afford a vacation. I'm here to write the story on Uncle Yah Yah and then I must leave. However, if over the weekend you feel charitable, I would be most happy to accept any donations you may give—large or small. Believe me, it would mean the world to me." We both laughed.

"I can see that you're going to be a lot of fun, Rudy."

"I certainly hope so."

"Well, I must go and tell Uncle Yah Yah that you're here."

"You're a friend of Uncle Yah Yah's?"

"All I need to do is move my clothes and bed. You could then say that I lived with Uncle Yah Yah."

"Would you explain that a little?"

"Whenever I'm not working, I spend all my free time at Uncle Yah Yah's house. He and Aunt Willie Mae are like parents to me. I eat all my meals there, and being that this is the busiest time of the season, I help cook, clean and do the shopping because it's too much for Aunt Willie Mae to handle by herself."

"I see, but I'm still a little confused. Isn't Uncle Yah Yah some kind of spiritual teacher?"

"Yes, he's a teacher. He taught me the difference between an education and indoctrination."

"Listen Freda, do you have to leave right now? I would like to ask you some questions about Uncle Yah Yah, and you would be very helpful if you could stay awhile."

"Yeah, I'll stay awhile. But are you sure that's all you want?"

"Okay. First business and then pleasure."

"She laughed, sat down, and then crossed her lovely legs. I grabbed for my notes and sat down in front of her knees, which looked like Cadillac hubcaps to me.

"Now, let's see. Will you tell me what it was that Uncle Yah Yah taught you about education?"

"I will explain that. But didn't you say you were confused?" What are you confused about?"

"I was wondering if Uncle Yah Yah knew about you."

"You mean does he know that I'm a prostitute? Yes. As a matter of fact, he's the one who started me in earnest."

"You mean Uncle Yah Yah is..."

"No. I don't mean that Uncle Yah Yah took me to bed. And if he did I wouldn't tell you, but I do mean he put my head straight. Let me start from the beginning."

"Please do."

"O.K. I told you how I got started two years ago as a

prostitute, but I didn't tell you it wasn't all peaches and cream. I thought that I could turn a few secret tricks, get some much needed money, and go back to school with what happened in the dark and forgotten. But like the old saying goes, 'What's done in the dark, soon comes to light." That was something I hadn't anticipated. The other students started avoiding me. They cut conversations short when I came around them. That's when I began to feel like the worst person in the world. I felt stupid for letting myself fall to such a low state. I began to think about suicide.

"One morning about 5:00 a.m., I went over to the lake and walked out on the narrow pier. The water is deep at the end of the pier. Since I can't swim I'd decided to jump, but thought I'd sit a minute before jumping. I started crying uncontrollably. Then I felt someone next to me. It was Uncle Yah Yah. He didn't say a word. He just sat down, put his arm around me, and pressed my head on his chest.

"Somehow I felt that he knew why I was crying and he understood. I started talking between sobs. I told him everything that had brought me to that point of trying to kill myself. I told him how ashamed I was because of my two years of college and my intentions to become a teacher, that I let myself down and I should've known better.

"After I had cried and talked myself out of jumping, Uncle Yah Yah stood up and pulled me to my feet, took my hand and let me to his house. He didn't say a word all that time and didn't say anything until we entered the house. He called to his wife to bring coffee for two. His town of voice was jovial. Not at all serious or giving any hint that my world had almost just come to an end. In a way I was happy that he didn't let on that I had a problem, because I didn't want to tell anyone else my story. But then too, I was thinking that he hadn't taken my problem seriously.

"Aunt Willie Mae brought the coffee, exchanged greetings, and left the room. I know now that she knew Uncle Yah Yah was handling a serious matter. He encouraged me to drink my coffee and then announced that there was nothing wrong with me. He said that I had more reasons to be happy than sad because I was at the forkroad of my life, which everyone must face sooner or later.

"He said, "The fork in the road is the point where you must decide whether you will take the path of the many and do as society wants you to do, or take that path of the few and do as you want to do."

"He further said, 'You didn't want to kill yourself.' You were acting in accordance with what you believed society thought of you. You're now at the fork in the road. One path leads to selfishness and suffering, the other path leads to greatness and the uplifting of humanity. The younger you are when you come to this fork in the road, the greater you will be, regardless of the path you choose. You will be an example one way or the other.

"God in His mercy has put two guides at the fork in the road. One is good and the other is evil. They both call you to their path, but you must choose. The noblest thing a person can do is to dedicate himself to the uplifting of humanity. So what do you want to do in life?" I told him that I wanted to be a school teacher, but now I doubted if I could get a job anywhere.

"He said, 'A person as young and with as much potential as I, could buy my own school and hire her own teachers, because God helps those who desire to help His people.

"I asked him what God thought of prostitution? He said, 'God only recognizes good, so if your intentions are good, then that's all that God sees.' He told me that no one is held accountable for the things that they do without a cause or purpose.

"He went on to tell me, 'You have no education. Education comes only after you come to the fork in the road and choose a guide. Then your education begins. Education is the flying carpet that transports you to your goal in life. It puts you in motion. All the instructions you receive before you know your purpose in life are only indoctrinations—you can't do anything with it.'

"He told me about the prostitute that Jesus would not condemn and about the prostitute in the story of Joshua at the battle of Jericho. Then he said that I reminded him of the queen ant. 'The queen ant at the time of her marriage flight; he said 'has sex with as many males as she come in contact with. Then she flies off to find a place to build a nest. She then clips her own wings, lay eggs and start a whole new ant colony all by herself. God loves her because *her efforts are for the preservation of her kind!*

"Well, to make a long story short, I couldn't sleep that night. I kept thinking of what Uncle Yah Yah had said about me getting my own school. I had to laugh, because I saw that if I could afford a school, it would have to be a very little one. That's when it hit me. My whole purpose in life. Everything went through my mind like a flash, and it was so real that I cried. I was so happy. It was all as plain as day. I would work at what I was doing and save the money I'd need, or at least enough to open a day care center with kindergarten.

I could hire my assistants and in a short time I would be able to expand to the fourth grade. That's all that I live for now and I can never forget Uncle Yah Yah for helping me to see what I'm all about. I have gained respect and friendship, and I'm proud of my success. Rudy, forgive me. You only asked me one question and I've been talking my head off."

"No, no. You're doing just fine. I need all the information I can get."

"Well, did I clear up some of the confusion?"

"Yes you did Freda, but don't let me stop you. What else did you want to say?"

"Only that a lot of people don't understand Uncle Yah Yah, and especially the preachers. They ran him out of the church one time because he was trying to get them to understand that we learn by our sins and we should not be condemned—but forgiven."

"Yeah, I was told that he was teaching the virtue of sin."

"You see what I mean, Rudy. That makes it sound like Uncle Yah Yah was trying to get everybody to go out and commit all the sin that they can, and that's not true."

"Just what was he saying that made them want to run him out?"

"I would rather have Uncle Yah Yah answer that one for you. However, I can assure you that my fate would've been sealed if I'd consulted one of those jive time preachers during my suicidal sojourn. He would've been of no help because he would not have wanted anyone to know that a whore was receiving any help from his holiness. The preachers have become so holy that they've forgotten they're supposed to be in the street to save the sinner. They lock themselves and their congregation behind closed doors and swear opposition to the sinner, the very man God wants. Naturally, they are against Uncle Yah Yah."

There was a knock on the door.

"Come in," I said. A brother dressed like a waiter came in the room.

"Room service, Mr. Hawkins. Hi Freda, what's happening?"

"Hi brother-in-law dear. Rudy, this is Will Fortny, Uncle Yah Yah's great nephew. Everybody calls him brother-in-law dear because he married Mrs. Walters' daughter Sue, the receptionist."

"Pleased to meet you, brother-in-law."

"Same here. I hear that you're writing a story on Uncle Yah Yah."

"Yes, and I was getting some very helpful information from Freda. Maybe before it's over with I'll get around to you."

"Sure thing. I'd be glad to help. I came up to see if you wanted room service, or are you coming to the dining room? Here's the menu. Mrs. Walters says that you're her guest and that everything is on the house."

"Hey. That's great. Tell Mrs. Walters that I'm grateful for her kindness. I don't know if I'll come to dinner, but what time does it start?"

"From five to seven," said brother-in-law.

"Freda. How much longer can you stay?" I asked.

"I think I'd better be going now. It's almost five o'clock."

"In that case, I'll be coming to the dining room brother-in-law. Also, I'll be looking forward to talking with you before I interview the old man."

"What old man?" Freda asked.

Before I could answer, brother-in-law said, "Don't say that to his face, or you might get a right hand across the chin. Right Freda?"

"You've got that right brother-in-law dear."

They both laughed, but noticing the baffled look on my face, brother-in-law said, "No joke. That old man will knock you out. Tell him Freda. Tell him about the guy who ripped off that little girl last summer, who Uncle Yah Yah knocked out."

"It's true. Two other girls and me saw the whole thing. He knocked that guy out right in front of the women's quarters."

"Will you tell me how it all came about? If you have the time, of course."

Freda looked at her watch and said, "Yes, it happened like this. A little ten year old girl became very friendly with a man about forty. At first the girl's mother thought it was cute, until one day the daughter was missing for about three hours. The mother searched everywhere, but could not find her daughter. Finally the girl showed up. Her clothes were dirty, pine needles in her hair, and she was walking with apparent difficulty. Her mother asked her where she'd been and the girl lied, but the mother examined her and found blood on her underwear. She made the girl tell the truth. The man had raped her in the woods and told her not to tell. Mrs. Walters called the State Troopers, but before they came, the child molester tried to leave. That's when Uncle Yah Yah stood by his car to prevent him from leaving. The man tried to push Uncle Yah Yah aside and that's when Uncle Yah Yah knocked him out with just one punch. So you'd better watch your mouth when you go to interview Uncle Yah Yah."

"I'll remember that. It was nice meeting you brother-in-law, I'll be looking to talk with you—say tomorrow?"

"That's cool with me."

"O.K. And thank you, Freda. You've been a big help."

"Think nothing of it. I'll see you around," she said as they both left the room.

I looked over my notes and discovered that there were still a lot of questions yet to be answered concerning Uncle Yah Yah. I still didn't know his full name, where he received his education, how old he was, the basis of his philosophy, and it seemed as though I'd have a book before it was over with.

## Chapter Five

## ROSALYN AND BRENDA

**DINNER WAS DELICIOUS.  THE BISCUITS SEEMED** to melt in my mouth, and it turned out to be a rewarding experience to boot.  I met two sisters.  Both of them were pretty as a picture.  They saw I was alone so they invited me to join them at their table.  I was more than glad to accept the offer.

Brenda seemed to be the talker of the two.  She told me of the fun that they'd had swimming and dancing all week.  It wasn't long before they got around to telling me of their visit with Uncle Yah Yah. I informed them that I was writing a story about Uncle Yah Yah and would appreciate it if they would tell me about their visit with him.

Brenda broke into blushing laughter and said, "We talked to Uncle Yah Yah about the sex revolution."  Rosalyn took it from there, and with excitement glowing in her eyes, she said, "Yeah. I asked him what he thought about the Sex Revolution, I just wanted to see how he would react to it. You know how religious people never want to deal with that subject. I just wanted to see if he could handle it."

"Well, what happened? Did he discuss it with you?"

Brenda said, "He sure did, and I discovered that Uncle Yah Yah is a hip old man."

"Exactly what were your questions?"

Brenda said, "Rosalyn asked him at what age did he think young people should become sexually involved with one another. He told her that 'Girls should start at the age of eleven or twelve because that's about the average age of puberty and boys should start about thirteen or fourteen.' Then Rosalyn asked him if that wasn't a little too young? He said, 'God says that they should marry when nature prepared them to have children. The people of the Asiatic civilizations recognize this, but European civilizations are bent on keeping their sons and daughters children as long as possible. You cannot suppress the sexual urges in the youth without causing great harm to the mentality of the youth. One look at the mental institutions in this country will demonstrate the great need to change these old Victorian sex laws.'

"After that, Rosalyn was speechless," said Brenda. "So I asked him what about promiscuity and sex in the movies, television, and class rooms. I wanted to know if he thought this Sex Revolution was going a little too far, or did he see any good coming out of it?" He said, "It's the best thing that could've happened. Young people are now discovering for themselves what sex is all about. Of course, some mistakes will be made, like any other

48

experiment, but I believe that eventually they'll discover the hidden secrets.' I asked him what are the hidden secrets and he said, without going into detail, 'That at one time, far back in history, sex was understood to be sacred or holy and was practiced with that attitude. Holy sexual union is strengthening and the quickest way of achieving the highest mental and physical states. But over the ages this knowledge was lost to the masses, and the elite or ruling class kept the secret to themselves. The young people of today are well on their way towards discovering this truth. By learning what sex is NOT, they must learn what sex IS.' We were surprised at Uncle Yah Yah's answers, but we were glad that we asked those questions. Now we know that Uncle Yah Yah is a very serious person and is not to be played with." Brenda concluded.

We sat there talking a while longer about the fun to be had at the resort, and before we left the dining room they invited me to a party at their cabin that night. Again, I gladly accepted.

I was anxious to get the interview with Mrs. Sally Walters over with, but it was only six thirty. I still had an hour to wait. I noticed a phone booth next to a gift shop, so I decided to call my wife.

"Georgia. It's me what's happening?"

"There is nothing going on here. I was just waiting for you to call so I could tell you about you're out whoring around."

"Me? Girl you should be ashamed of yourself, defaming my good name and character like that, and in the public, too."

"What public?"

"You know everybody listens to these telephones. What about Watergate?"

"Who do you think you're fooling, Rudy? Don't you try that weak stuff on me, I know you're whoring around up there."

"I just got here. I haven't even unpacked my bags yet. Who do you think I am, the fastest John in the east or something? Hey Sugar Lump, do you still love me?"

"Yes, I love you, Rudy, but you don't love me. You don't even know it's our fifteenth anniversary."

"Listen sweety. I know it. I just momentarily forgot, that's all.

"You're momentarily lying, Rudy. When is it, if you know?"

"O.K. You got me. But don't start up or I'll take back the gift I bought you."

"You bought me a gift? Sweetheart, you're the best husband in the whole world, and I take back all the bad things I've said about you. What did you get me, lover?"

"Well, I haven't got it yet. But "I'm going to get it as soon as you tell me the date of our anniversary."

"It's tomorrow, wise guy. You're a jive Pittsburgh farmer and you'd better bring me a gift when you come home. When are you coming home?"

"Do you miss me, Sugar?"

"Yes I do."

"Girl, you ought to cut that stuff out. I haven't been gone one day yet."

"What you gonna buy me?"

"I'm going to the gift shop and buy you a big Teddy Bear, as soon as I hang up this phone. See how much I love you?"

"You promise?"

"Sure I promise. Now give me a little kiss over the phone."

"Are you ready to tell me about how the ladies are treating you?"

"You got me all wrong, Sugar Mama."

"Don't you Sugar Mama me. What about those women?"

"Be cool. Don't shout. How's my children?"

"The women Rudy."

"Okay, okay! Listen, I just had dinner with two of the prettiest things you ever set eyes on. They're sisters, nineteen and twenty. They've invited me to come to a party in their cabin tonight, and I'm going to take the nineteen year-old to bed first. Now, what've you got to say to that?"

"I think you're the biggest liar in the world. Did you see Uncle Yah Yah yet?"

"Not yet."

"Do me a favor. Ask him what he thinks about the Women's Liberation Movement, and don't forget."

"Okay. I'll do that. I should be home Sunday night."

"If you're not here Sunday night by twelve o'clock, I'm calling the police and putting a missing persons out on you, Mr. Whore Master. And if you forget my Teddy Bear, you're gonna get beat up. You hear me?"

"Yes, sweet Sugar Lump."

"Are you going to call me tomorrow?

"Yes sir, master sergeant mama."

"What time, wise guy?"

"About five o'clock p.m. And listen, if anything should go wrong with you and the children, you be sure to call my lawyer, Ted Gastto, O.K.?"

"Rudy, what could go wrong? You're only going to be gone for two days."

"Just do as I say. I've got to go now, sweety. You be cool and kiss the babies for me, O.K.?"

"Alright, you too. Bye, bye."

I had planned to take Georgia and the children to visit relatives in Florida, but here I was still working. I went to the gift shop and bought a big Teddy Bear that was white and black, and took it to my cabin.

## Chapter Six

### MRS. SALLY WALTERS

**IT WAS 7:30 P.M. WHEN I WALKED INTO THE OFFICE** for my meeting with Mrs. Walters, and sure enough, she was there waiting for me. I got right down to the business of clearing up my list of questions.

"Mrs. Walters, what is Uncle Yah Yah's real or full name?"

"His name is Paul Walters."

"Is he related to you?"

"Yes. He's my uncle."

"That's right. Freda told me that Sue was his great niece. I didn't even recognize what she was saying. Can you tell me how old he is?"

"Yes he is 72. My father is three years older than Uncle Yah Yah. Grandpa Jeffre had two sons and my father was the oldest."

"Mrs. Walters, do you own all of this property? How many acres are there?"

"This property belongs to the Walters family. It's 175 acres. Grandpa Jeffre inherited this property from Master Walters when he died in 1910. Grandpa Jeffre and Master Walters were the last descendants of a family of masters and slaves. Even though slavery had been abolished, long before Master Walters and my Grandpa were born. The situation in these parts remained pretty much the same for a long time after. Mostly because the family of slaves-consisting of our great, great grandparents-considered themselves free."

"I see. And can you tell me where Uncle Yah Yah received his education?"

"Uncle Yah Yah didn't go to school. Grandpa Jeffre taught him to read and to write and he took it from there. Now you are probably going to ask me who taught Grand-pa Jeffre."

"Yes, I was wondering about that. Do you know?"

"Well, it's like this. Master Walters was a 33 and 1/3 degree Mason. After the last members of the family died, he had Grandpa Jeffre bring his wife and two sons to live with him in the big house. Master Walters had a large library in the big house, but he wouldn't let anyone go in there but Grandpa. He taught Grandpa to read, write, and about Masonry. They used to spend a lot of time researching books together. Also, Master Walters would take Grandpa Jeffre up to the cabin on the hill. They would stay sometimes as long as three and four weeks, practicing Masonic rituals, fasting and studying. After Master Walters died, Grandpa Jeffre began to take Uncle Yah Yah to the library and to the cabin, and that's how he received his education. Uncle Yah Yah still uses that old cabin every now and then."

"Where did he get the name Uncle Yah Yah, and what does it mean?"

Grandpa Jeffre gave it to him. I think it means 'he will not be overcome by sin.'

"I was told that Uncle Yah Yah retreated to the cabin after he had been put out of the church. Can you tell me anything about this?"

"Uncle Yah Yah was never a member of a church. He was invited to speak at a church by some friends once, and that's when he was stopped in the middle of his speech and asked to leave. But that had nothing to do with him retreating to the cabin. In fact, the church incident took place in 1950 and it was in 1952 when Uncle Yah Yah moved into the cabin to stay."

"Why did he want to live in the cabin?"

"He received a revelation."

"He what?"

Uncle Yah Yah used to pray in the library at the big house. One night he called us together and told us that God had answered his prayers. He said that God told him that he would not have to go in search of the sheep, because God would send them (the sheep) to him to be fed with the truth, and that God would establish him with heaven on earth as a reward for his services.

"At first we thought that Uncle Yah Yah was losing his mind, but we soon saw for ourselves the truth of his revelation. He moved into the cabin and shortly after that people began to come up here. It was strange, because we never had visitors in these parts. But suddenly people began to show interest in hiking and picnicking on the hill where Uncle Yah Yah was living in the cabin. The strangest part of it all was that most of these people were black. Soon people were coming just to see Uncle Yah Yah.

"All this took place between the years 1952 and 1953. I never will forget, because I was pregnant with Sue at that time and the family was trying to make me marry Eddy- Sue's father. Uncle Yah Yah sent for me one day and asked me if I'd wanted to marry Eddy. I told him that I didn't. He told me to tell the family that he had some important work for me to do, and that I wasn't going to marry Eddy. Nobody said a word about me getting married after that. That's when Uncle Yah Yah gave me his plans to build this resort. He named it Paradise Gardens, and he said that God told him that as long as he continued to teach the truth, the resort would be successful, and it has. So now you know why we all believe in him."

"What does Uncle Yah Yah call his religion?"

"He doesn't call it anything. He says he believes in love."

"Does he have a Bible?"

"He believes in all Bibles, all prophets, and the truth wherever it can be found."

"How long did he live in the cabin? I mean before he moved into his present house?"

"About three years. He moved after he married Willie Mae. She's his second wife. His first wife died in 1947 from a stroke. He has two children by his first wife and two by Willie Mae. The oldest are married and the two youngest are in college. You should ask Willie Mae to tell you how she met and married Uncle Yah Yah. I think you'll find her story interesting."

"Thank you, I'll ask her. Is there anything else you'd like to tell me about Uncle Yah Yah?"

"Not if you don't have any more questions."

"Well, I still have two more days to be here, so if I come up with any more questions, I'll be back, O.K.?"

"Alright, sweetheart. Stop in to see me whenever you like."

I thanked her again for everything and left. In my cabin I remembered the party that Rosalyn and Brenda had invited me to. For some unknown reason, I just didn't feel like going, but I'd promised them that I'd come. I cleaned up a little and started for the party at cabin number seven.

Paradise Gardens looks like a carnival at night. Colored lights are hung all over the place and the atmosphere was exciting- like Coney Island.

The party was well on the way when I got there. Brenda grabbed me by the arm and introduced me around. People were smoking that smoke, drinking, and dancing, but I wasn't in the mood for it. So I stayed just long enough not to look conspicuous when I left.

I went straight to bed and was almost asleep when the door began to rattle. I opened the door, in walked

Rosalyn as she said, "That Party's going to last all night and I'm tired."

With that said, she took off her clothes and crawled in the bed. I started to say something dumb, like "you can't sleep here," but I caught myself. There was only one thing for me to do. So I summoned up all the strength that was in me, stuck out my chest and went to bed.

I yawned myself awake at 10:30 Saturday morning and found a note on the pillow instead of Rosalyn. The note said that she'd see me at dinner.

## Chapter Seven

### BROTHER –IN- LAW DEAR

**I CRAWLED OUT OF BED, WASHED, SHAVED,** dressed, and was preparing to go in search of some coffee when Brother-in-law Dear arrived with a breakfast tray. I could've kissed him.

He had a few minutes to talk so I asked him what he thought about Uncle Yah Yah.

He said, "I think Uncle Yah Yah is a God in his own right. He has created a heaven for himself here on earth. He has peace and he teaches peace to others. I know that he says all men are Gods, but he also says that you have to recognize it in yourself. So Uncle Yah Yah is my example of peace love and graciousness."

"Are there many who believe as you, concerning Uncle Yah Yah?"

"Yes. But he's against building churches and keeping a large number of followers around him. He says that our duty, once we know the truth, is to go among our people who need us the most, and teach the truth to whoever wants to hear it."

"From what I hear, Uncle Yah Yah's teachings are far from winning a popularity contest. Is that true?"

"Uncle Yah Yah taught us that if we teach the truth, the foolish will hate us, and if we don't teach it, the wise will hate us. So, we just try to please God, that's all."

We left my cabin together. He went back to the kitchen and I started for Uncle Yah Yah's house.

## Chapter Eight

## AUNT WILLIE MAE

**IT WAS 11:15 A.M. WHEN I CROSSED THE TENNIS** court on my way back to Uncle Yah Yah's house. The resort really did look and feel like paradise. I breathed in the fresh air and it was like a cool drink of water satiating a parched tongue. My walk came to an end too soon.

It was a pretty ranch style house made of red brick. I rang the bell and was told to come in. I opened the screen door and walked into the cool air of an air-conditioned conventionally furnished shangolla. I felt at home the moment I walked in.

"Good morning, my name is Rudy Hawkins. I'm a reporter from the Essex News Weekly, and I'm here to write an article about Uncle Yah Yah."

"Come in and have a seat. I'm Uncle Yah Yah's wife. My name is Willie Mae. We have been expecting you. Freda told us that you were here yesterday."

Willie Mae was a small woman with a tan complexion, and if looks were the judge, she didn't look a day over thirty. She told me she was fifty.

"Yes, Freda told me a lot about you and Uncle Yah Yah. She loves you a lot."

"We love Freda a lot."

"I also had to talk with your niece, Mrs. Sally Walters, and she told me to ask you to tell me about your meeting and marriage to Uncle Yah Yah."

"I'd be glad to tell you all about that. But first, let me give you this."

She placed a large brown envelope in my hand and said, "I have been praying some day we would be able to get this published. Its some short stories and essays that Uncle Yah Yah wrote. I saved them and when we learned that you were coming, I typed as much as of his material as I could find. Also, I might as well tell you that Uncle Yah Yah doesn't like reporters. We had a very hard time getting him to see you, so don't expect too much out of him."

"This looks like a lot of material. It might even be enough to be a book, but it's not up to me when it comes to getting it published. I'll take it but I can't promise you anything, Mrs. Walters."

"Well, I'm giving it to you. You get it published, O.K.?"

"Alright, I'll do my best. What does Uncle Yah Yah

have against reporters?"

"He says that most of you are afraid to print the truth, and he feels it's a waste of time talking to someone who's going to take what he says and turn it around to mean other than what he said."

"I can understand that, but is he going to see me?

"Oh, he'll see you, but don't look for him to have too much to say. Now, you wanted to know about the story of Uncle Yah Yah's and my marriage."

"Yes I would."

"Well, it happened like this. I came here with some friends to spend a few days. We all went up to the cabin to see Uncle YahYah. I knew that he was my husband the moment I saw him. I didn't say anything to anyone, but I just knew. We talked with him for a while and when it was time to leave, I didn't want to go. I didn't say anything or show any signs of what I was feeling inside, but Uncle Yah Yah knew. He pointed to me and said, 'Hurry home and hurry back, don't keep me waiting.' That was all I needed to hear. I went home, got my things, and I didn't even try to explain to my folks what I was doing. I came back to the cabin, and a week or two later we were married."

"That's all there was to it?"

"Not exactly. Three months before I came to the resort, Uncle Yah Yah informed members of his family that he was going to get married again, and that he was sending for his spiritual wife. He gave them a written description of what this new wife would look like. Then he told his niece, Sally, to put it up for safekeeping. When I arrived, they thought they were seeing a ghost, because I fitted the description so well."

"I can see now why your niece wanted me to hear that story, and I agree with her, it's strange. Where is Uncle Yah Yah now?"

"He's out back with some of our young friends. Come on, I'll take you to him."

**Chapter Nine**

**UNCLE YAH YAH**

**OUT BACK UNCLE YAH YAH WAS SITTING AT A** table, in the shade of a large beach umbrella, with two young ladies and a man. They looked to be in their early twenties. I was shocked to see that Uncle Yah Yah looked more like a dapper Dan, or a whiskered Pete than a sage, and he didn't appear to be a day over forty. He was a handsome man and his curly, black hair sprinkled with gray, reminded me of the late Adam Clayton Powell.

"Uncle Yah Yah, this is Mr. Hawkins from the newspaper."

"Good. Sit down Mr. Hawkins. We have been expecting you. Pour yourself a glass of fruit juice. I'll be with you in a minute. Now, what was I saying Elna?"

Mrs. Walters went back into the house. I sat down and got set to take notes. The young woman named Elna said, "You were saying that I'm selfish, don't you remember? You must be getting old Uncle Yah Yah."

"Oh, I remember. I just wanted to see if what I was saying was going in one ear and out the other."

Everyone laughed, then Uncle Yah Yah said, "But before I prove my point, let me introduce you to Mr. Hawkins. This is Elna, Ann and Robert."

Everyone said "pleased to meet you," and Uncle Yah Yah turned to speak to Elna again.

"Yes. I said you are selfish. I know you don't want to accept that, but it's true. You told me that you're a professional woman, free, and independent. And when I said that a beautiful young woman such as you should be married, you said you didn't need a man to take care of you because you're capable of taking care of yourself. Is that right, or did I forget anything?"

"No, you haven't forgotten anything."

"O.K. If you don't want to get married, then why don't you have a child?"

"Have a child! Without being married?"

"Now you think that Uncle Yah Yah is trying to get you to violate the law, but I'm only trying to show you how selfish you are. Look at yourself. You're in the prime of your life, free and independent. Would you say that to be young, free and independent is a valuable state of being and worth passing on to future generations?"

"Of course. But you still haven't told me why you say I'm selfish."

"I'm saying that if you have as good a thing as you say, then offer some of that good to future generations. If you had a child-and you look like you could produce a strong son-you could share your good fortune of freedom and independence with him. He would grow up and to be a great man. Then you would have performed a true service to mankind. Ah, no pun intended."

We all laughed and I noticed that Uncle Yah Yah had a comical way of expressing himself that kept his listeners laughing.

"To raise a child you need two parents," Elna said.

"That's the second time you've brought man's law into this. First, you said that having a child out of wedlock is against the law, but in Mary's day (Jesus' mother) the penalty was death. What did God think of man's law at that time? Second, who said you had to have two parents to raise a child, God or man? Who raised Ishmael? Hagar raised him and she did a mighty good job of it too. Ishmael, son of Abraham and a prophet. What about the poor widow's son whom the prophet Elijah resurrected. And King Solomon, the son of a handmaid? I'm not telling you to go to jail, I'm telling you to serve God. Because it is He that has given you all the good that you now have and enjoy. You're made for the purpose of reproduction, and to pass on to future generations the best that is in you. That's God's law. What I'm trying to show you might sound strange to the rest of you, but keep in mind that I'm directing this to the independent Miss Elna."

"Uncle Yah Yah, you're making feel like I'm the worst person in the world."

"Does that mean that you're going to bring me a baby the next time you come to see me?"

"You know that I can't promise you that, Uncle Yah Yah."

"Well, do you understand what I'm trying to tell you concerning God's law?"

"Yes, I do."

"Then that's better than a promise. I'll let you alone for now. Tell me, Ann. How long have you and Robert been married?"

Ann looked at her husband and smiled, then she said, "One year and three months."

"Are you happy?"

"Yes, we are Uncle Yah Yah."

"See what you're missing Elna?"

"Hey. I thought you said you were going to leave me alone for awhile?" Elna said in a little girlish manner.

"That's right, I forgot."

Everyone laughed and Uncle Yah Yah turned to me and said, "Mr. Hawkins, I don't want to take up too much of your time, I know that you're here on business. Did my wife give you the material I wrote?"

"Yes, I have it right here."

"Then all I have to say is in those writings. I

just hope that you print it just as it is and don't change any of it."

"I can promise you that I won't change any of it. I'm just a reporter and I'll take it just like you give it to me."

"Is there anything else that I can do for you?"

I wasn't prepared for a brush off, but that's what I was getting. I still had a few questions to ask, so I figured that maybe if I asked him a question or two, he'd soften up a bit.

"I have a few questions to ask you, Uncle Yah Yah, if I may?"

"Personal questions, or questions for the article?"

"For the article."

"All I have to say to the newspapers is in that stack of materials my wife gave you. I have nothing else to make known to the public."

Feeling kind of mixed up, and not wanting to make a fool of myself, I said, "Well in that case my work is done, but I do have one personal question that my wife wanted me to ask you. She wants to know what do you think about the Women's Liberation Movement."

"For your wife, I'll do my best to answer that. The first things that come to mind to the average person, when we say Women's Liberation Movement, are: job discrimination, equal wages, fair opportunity in education and politics. These are not the real issues. They're only the outer signs of an internal conflict. Most people look at the material manifestation and accept that as reality. But appearance is not reality, it's only the result of the creation of the mind. When we look past the matter to see what caused it to be, then we are seeing true reality. As a man thinks, so he causes it to be."

"The fruit tree is a perfect example of easy we misunderstand reality. We think that the fruit tree's purpose is only to produce fruit for us to eat, but the tree has another idea of its importance. The tree creates a sweet fruit and hides its seed in it. We are attracted by the fruit and unknowingly help fulfill the true purpose of the tree, which is the spreading of its seed far and wide. The true purpose of the tree is the seed, not the fruit."

"So it is with the Women's Liberation Movement. I deal with the spiritual side of life, so I will not speak on the outer appearances, such as jobs, education, and equal opportunity."

"The woman has always functioned as she should. It is we, the men, who are out of order. Man has forgotten that his woman is the Goddess through whom he reproduces the Gods. Woman has always stimulated growth and change in the physical and mental condition of man."

" Since the beginning of time, when Eve provoked Adam to eat of the tree of knowledge, woman's role has been the same. It wasn't until Adam ate of the tree that things began to happen. They discovered the secret of holy union, which made them as Gods. They left the garden to multiply and inhabit the earth until the day that God established on earth as it is in heaven. During this time the knowledge of holy union and the secret that man is God, would be lost, only to re-emerge at the Day of Judgment. That is why it says in the Psalms, 82:1, 8, "God, standeth in the congregation of the mighty: He judgeth among the gods.' Verse 8, 'Arise, O God, judge the earth: for thou shalt inherit all nations.' Verse 6, says, "I have said, Ye are gods and all of you are children of the most high."

"Tell your wife that there is nothing wrong with the women. They have always done their part and are beautiful. It is the man who is in trouble, because he has lost contact with the God that is in him. I see the Women's Liberation Movement as an attempt to awaken her sleeping God. She knows that she is a Goddess, and like it was in the beginning, Eve is offering Adam the apple.

"Does that sound strange to you?" Well, it's the truth."

"Yes, Uncle YahYah. That's the first time I've heard the story of Adam and Eve told like that, and I'll tell that to my wife just the way you told it to me."

"You do that, and when you can get away from work for a few days, feel free to come to visit us again," Uncle YahYah said as he extended his hand, indicating that my interview was over. I didn't want to leave, but being that I had the manuscript, I figured that the best thing to do was take a look at it, and if I wasn't satisfied, then I would come back for some more information.

"Thank you Uncle YahYah. It was a pleasure to meet you. I'd better be going now," I said as I shook his hand, and after saying good-bye to everyone, I left.

Back in my cabin, I opened Uncle Yah Yah's manuscript and began to read.

UNCLE YAH YAH'S
MANUSCRIPT

Chapter Ten

THE MANUSCRIPT

By

Uncle Yah Yah

*It is better to have what is in this little book and not need it, than to need what is in it and not have it.*

-*Uncle Yah Yah*

## CONTENTS

## INTRODUCTION

**I AM UNCLE YAH YAH AND I HAVE SOMETHING** to say to you. I must have my say. Whether the fools accept these small truths or not-I could care less. This message is for my kin folk, The Wise Ones, who have waited for me to trumpet this call to higher consciousness for more than 400 years.

Some of you will reject my words on first sight, without so much as a second glance. To you I say just one word, Fool! But for those of you who have the courage to at least, sniff at my words before proclaiming that they stink, I offer you three important pieces of knowledge. The first knowledge is of society, the second is of religion and the third is the knowledge of self.

It is to you courageous ones that I write these words of wisdom. The weakhearted can't endure this fact-finding trip we are about to embark upon.

The weakhearted are silly people afraid of their own shadows. Whenever challenges raises its shaggy head, the poor cowards tremble and take flight, unaware that discovery is the fruit of life. The fools dive headlong into the arms of the death that they think they are running from. Fear to learn new things is the worst kind of death.

But let us leave the weakhearted chained to their fear and ignorance. We have no time to waste discussing fools. In fact, the wisdom of a wise man can be measured in the swiftness he displays in shunning the fools. So let us hurry into what matters.

Knowledge is power. The world is divided between those who know and those who know not. Failure to pursue knowledge makes man a slave. Society and religion are the main slave holders. Knowledge will give you the power to overcome these two taskmasters, and knowledge will set you free to establish your own identity. "Know truth and go free."

Many of you still think that knowledge is confined to certain institutions of learning. You are quick to ask, "What's your alma mater?" Knowledge is not the slave of Harvard, Oxford, or Yale, but he is a freeman and chooses his own associates. Those who walk with knowledge soon become bored with what is common or ordinary. Because of their discontent, they are labeled savior, madman, Satan, or all of the three.

There is no set course to take to find knowledge; each man must search for himself. Sometimes a single word or phrase can break through the veil of ignorance and bring you face to face with knowledge. It's your responsibility to establish a lasting communication with him. For his favors, knowledge has but one obligation. That is, you must make known what you learn from him. "Teach in order to learn."

You may question my reasons for arranging the three powers in the order of Society, Identity, and Religion. That is a very good question and my very good answer is that is that I have no reason for it. It doesn't matter in what order you acquire this knowledge, but you can't reach perfection unless you master all three. If you think that to be strange, let me remind you that the greatest confusion is sometimes caused by the simplest truth.

In my explanation of Society, Identity, and Religion, I want you to keep in mind that this is the world as seen through the eyes of Uncle Yah Yah, not B.F. Skinner, Pavlov, Huxley, or Kant. This is Uncle Yah Yah's theory. Your heart will tell you if it's true.

I tell short stories and use animals, mostly to show some of the great lessons of life. Each story ends with a wise saying as to give you something to think about. Once you understand it's meaning, it will stick with you. A hint to the wise is sufficient. Don't be fooled by the simplicity of my choice of characters. Remember that what is said in a joke has a unique way of becoming a reality.

## SOCIETY

What is society? We think of society as a group of people united together for a common cause, standard, or pursuit of happiness.

Most of you will agree with that definition, but it's on this point that I offer my first argument. Take the statement of 'Unity on a common basis.' Here is one of the most misunderstood dictates of modern times. It reminds me of the little story of the intelligent mouse.

This little story illustrates the folly of accepting unity on face value.

## THE WISE LITTLE MOUSE

It was Sunday and the family had gone to visit with grandma, leaving the house empty except for Rudolph the cat. As usual, he was hungry and was stealing through all the rooms in hopes of finding a mouse.

Just as he entered the kitchen, right there, before his very eyes stood Swifty the intelligent mouse. Now Rudy sized up the situation as fast as he could and figured that the best way to get close enough to get his hands on Swifty, would be to use some tact.

Wagging his tail charmingly, speaking pleasantly, Rudy said, "Oh, how nice it is to see you, ah, Mr. Swifty. I was just thinking what a good thing it would be if we threw away our differences and came together on the basis of what we have in common. Now, logic dictates that we are both animals and live in the same house, so let us assemble our families in a show of unity and stop this fighting. Ah, what do you say to that?"

Swifty was cool and not the least bit taken in by this smooth talking, mouse eating trickster. Being wise from too many past narrow escapes, Swifty could see that Rudy, not only was hungry for leadership, but for mice too. So he knew just what he had to do.

Swifty said, "I find your suggestion very interesting. But logic, when it is misdirected, can be fatal. Such as assembling our families just because we live in the same house and are animals. That would be tragic to say the least. What we have in common is not enough to bring about unity. Unity comes only through leadership; and on the point of leadership, we cannot agree because I emphatically oppose to your leading me into the darkness of your digestive system."

Swifty then made a mad dash for his hole. Being safe, he called out, "Hey Rudy, whoever told you that togetherness constitutes unity?" Tell him I said he's a fool.

-End-

How often have we been lured by the call to unity only to satisfy the hunger of some vicious villain? They say, "Vote for me and I'll set you free!" So we unite, go to the polls, and set the villain free, who then becomes free, happy and rich. While you and I return to our poor homes and pitiful jobs. Where is the freedom in working for peanuts year in and year out? That reminds me of the story of the wolves.

*       *       *

## THE HUNGRY WOLVES

Two wolves stood on a hill, overlooking a herd of sheep, licking their wounds. Their attempt to steal a sheep or two had ended as a miserable failure; they got away with nothing except their behinds filled with the buckshots from the sheep herder's shot-gun.

Taking refuge on the hill and finding some shade from the noon day sun; one wolf said to his companion, "Look at what he did to my ass. He shot the hair off a spot on my butt, and it's all your fault."

His companion said as he tried to get a pellet out of his flank, "But I got shot too."

The wolf with the spot said, "Aw shut up. You said this job would be like taking candy from a baby, now just look at my behind. I won't be able to sit in that side for a year."

The companion said, "The sheep herder was supposed to be sleep, and how was I to know he had a gun?"

"Just shut your mouth," said the spotted wolf, "Your plans always go wrong. Just like the time you got us caught in the chicken coop. I guess that wasn't your fault either? So just shut up!
I don't want to hear nothing you've got to say. I'm so hungry I don't know what to do."

The companion said, "But I'm hungry too."

Spot said, I should have gone with my brother-in-law and sonny to hunt jack rabbits. But fool that I am, I let you talk me into this."

The companion laughed and said, "Chasing rabbits? Man you know that you're too old for that kind of stuff. Those rabbits are too fast for you. You would be too tired to eat by the time you caught one. Besides, one rabbit between three wolves ain't nothing."

Spot said, "Listen. I told you to shut your mouth, wise guy." Just then, something caught spot's eye. At the foot of the hill he saw sheep being chased by a familiar figure.

"Hey," said Spot to his companion, "Look down there. Ain't that cousin Willy? Man, Willy's stolen the whole herd. Let's go and help him. Hey cousin Willy!" Spot called out, "We're coming to help you, man."

The companion said, "Fool. You'd better be cool. If you go down there you'll have to fight for your life; and in your condition, I don't think you'd win."

"What are you talking about? Ain't that cousin Willy?" Spot asked.

"Yes, but Willy is working for the man, and he's the one who ratted on us in the first place. Didn't you hear him telling the man we were stealing sheep? He's helping the man take them back to the ranch."

"Well, I'll be damned. Working for the man, huh? Well I might work for the man too, if I could eat all I wanted. I'll bet Willy gets two sheep a week."

"No, Willy doesn't get any sheep. All he gets is milk and bread," said the companion.

"Not even a chop?" asked spot.

"No. And they keep him tied up at night."

"Well, I guess I've seen it all," said Spot as they prepared to go home. I just can't understand it. I would rather be shot in the behind and hungry-but free, than to be a willing slave for milk and bread."

-End-

We have become the slaves of society. Greedy politicians are like vultures. They only show up after society is dead. Society, in its true form, is a servant to the people. The people are under the direction of those in authority, and the peoples' welfare and protection must direct the actions of those in authority. That reminds me of the story about the lion.

## THE MAN, THE DONKEY, AND THE LION

One day while traveling through the wilderness, a man discovered a donkey grazing in an open field. He was very tired from carrying a heavy pack. Keeping his eyes on the donkey, he thought, "What luck. If I can catch this wild jack-ass I'll not have to carry this heavy bag."

So he started walking slowly toward the donkey, and to his great surprise the donkey began to walk towards him.

The donkey upon seeing the man thought to himself, "Oh, what good fortune. Here's a stray human, and if I can catch him he could get food and make shelter for me. If I should get sick, he could care for and protect me from danger."

So the man and the donkey went on their way through the wilderness, happy to have found each other.

Suddenly, a lion sprang upon them, holding them very firmly in a tight grip.

"What a good day this is. I was looking for one and found two," said the lion as he licked his chops in anticipation of dinner.

"Yes. You are fortunate to have two of us for your meal. But you should show some gratitude for such a blessing," said the donkey to the lion.

"What do you mean?" said the lion. I'm not ungrateful. I have never been ungrateful."

"Then free the master of the two of us and eat only the servant. Such an act would be proof that you are pious," the donkey said.

"Very good, I will do it. Now which of you is the master I will set the master free, but I will make my meal of the servant."

"Then let me go," said the man, "because it should be obvious to you that I am the master."

"Just a minute," interrupted the donkey. "I can clear up this dispute without a doubt."

The donkey then turned to the man and asked, "Who is it that feeds and shelters me?"

"I do," said the man.

"Who is it that would attend to me if I should get ill, and protect me from danger?"

"I would."

"Then it is settled," said the donkey, as he trotted off. But before he disappeared into the forest, the donkey turned and said,

"Remember, You Can Not Possess Without Being Possessed."

-End-

\*        \*        \*

There must be give and take from above and below. When that no longer exits, society dies.

People will not support the government unless they can see and feel the benefits of that government, such as better food, clothing, shelter, education, hospitals, welfare and the like. Have you noticed that we are having less and less to say about what society can and cannot do?

**PURSUIT OF HAPPINESS** is the next point I'd like

to deal with. Whose happiness are we pursuing? From my point of view we have no choice in the matter.

We are following the customs and traditions of our fore-fathers. Two hundred or more years ago our fathers established customs, traditions and a constitution. No doubt they were very happy pursuing that course of action. But what do you and I know of their real intent? Their reasons are lost to us forever. How can you be happy doing anything when you don't know what you are doing or why?

You say we found our fathers doing these things, so it is the ways of our civilization, and we follow in their footsteps-even if we prove, or have proof that our fathers were nuts. That reminds me of the story of the cats.

*     *     *

## THE FUNERAL OF THE CATS

The community cats were gathered at the foot of the willow tree, which was their habit when they had important matters to discuss. Today one of their fellow members had been run over by a speeding truck and they were trying to decide what to do with the dead member's remains.

Yellow Tom was the chairman of the board so he called the meeting to order. Raising himself to his full height, and glancing about to see if he had the attention of all the members, he said, "Fellow members. I would like to remind you that we have made much progress as a society of common house cats. That is, since we have been allied with the humans and civilization. We eat cooked food, and we speak the language of humans. All of this has given us a distinction that no other members of the cat family can claim."

The cats applauded.

Yellow Tom continued. "But there is still much room for improvement. At this very moment the carcass of one of our members lie rotting in the streets. This is very uncivilized. We must reform from such savagery."

The cats applauded.

Yellow Tom cleared his throat. "I suggest to you that we learn the funeral rites of the humans and that we should start practicing right now."

"What will we do?" the members wanted to know.

Tom said, "We will need some pretty flowers and we will sing some sad songs. We'll also need someone to cry and tell of the dead cat's good deeds."

"Just a minute," shouted an old cat from the rear of the crowd. "Isn't the death of our fellow enough, why should we kill the flowers? Sad music and crying will not help the dead and will no doubt, make some of us sick. Does it make any sense to speak all manner of good about him, now that he's dead, when most of us had nothing good to say of him while he was a live? Where do you get these strange ideas?" asked the old rebellious cat.

The crowd was quiet and all eyes were on Tom, as they waited for an answer.

"It's the way of civilization," said Yellow Tom, feeling a little confused.

"You call that civilization?" growled the old cat. Is it civilized to take up millions of acres of good land to store dead bodies, when the living are crowded because of the need for land? Is it civilized to take some of the best silks and satins and use them to line bronze coffins, while the living need clothes? Is it civilized to take set up beautiful marble stones all over the place to be forgotten in a few weeks, when they could've been used to construct something needed for the living? Well, what is your answer?"

Yellow Tom hung his head in shame and said. "I don't know."

"Well, I do," said the old cat, "Civilization is sometimes savage."

-End-

\*　　　　　\*　　　　　\*

Society has imprisoned all of you poor simple people, by imposing iron-like customs and traditions that trap you like animals in cages, called institutions of health, education, and the rest of the so-called governmental agencies.

If we go along with society's program we are considered perfectly normal and healthy people. But as soon as we begin to question the establishment, we become misfits as far as society is concerned.

Mental hospitals are full of people who had questions, some even had answers. But that's the price you pay when conformity becomes a bore. It makes you wonder if there is any escape. If you rebel you're dead, and if you don't you're dead.

The answer in a nut shell is to get knowledge of the rules and laws of society and then use those rules to fulfill your own purpose—without offending anyone.  This can only be done by those who have a very good understanding of what their aims and purposes are, and are sure of the world around them.  Such wise men are free.

Freedom doesn't come by changing one set of chains for another.  Freedom comes with knowledge of your purpose in life.  Then all things take on special meaning for you.  Freedom comes from within.  Like the story of the old man and they young rebels.

*   *   *

### FREEDOM

An old man was repairing the barn on his small farm when two young men, who were revolutionaries, came to speak with him.  The young rebels were smartly dressed in uniforms, and were carrying pamphlets with slogans written on them.

The first young man said, "Greetings old man and are you working hard?"

"Yes I am, and greetings to you also."

The second young man said, "It's a pity that you must work so hard at your age.  But don't worry, because tomorrow the revolution will bring you freedom."

"Free me.  What do you mean?" said the old man laughing.  "Would you free the birds from flying, or the fish from swimming?

What is this deprivation that you offer to me under the name of freedom?"

"Deprivation? Are you saying that we come to deprive you?" Asked the first of the two youths. "We have come to give you good news that you will soon be free, and instead of being happy, you say we come to deprive you. You should want to be free"

"I am already free. It is you who need to be free. Do you think that taking this government and having an opportunity to rule the people makes you free? That is not freedom, it is tyranny changing hands, the select few living and making themselves rich from the labor of the multitude of poor working people. I want no part of this sick illusion that you call freedom. So go away and leave me alone."

The two youths slowly walked away.

Freedom was never yesterday, nor will it ever be tomorrow.

**FREEDOM IS THE ETERNAL NOW.**

-End-

\*              \*              \*

Freedom is now, but only those who search out knowledge for themselves are wise enough to understand this fact. They don't wait for others to interpret reality for them. You can't live your own life as long as you are dependent upon others to tell you what you should do, and shouldn't do for your own well being.

If you don't know what's good for you, how the hell can someone else tell you?

The old man was free of politics and religion, and he was free from boredom. His knowledge made him free in the midst of captives. Because he searched for truths in order to find, or establish, his own awareness and identity, he was above the pettiness and sick illusions of society.

It's very foolish for a person to accept everything he hears on face value. That reminds me of the blackbird and the crane.

### IGNORAMUS, THE BLACK BIRD AND THE PROFESSOR

It had just stopped raining in the forest and the sky was rolling back a blanket of gray clouds. The sun had started to smile through the mist, and a beautiful rainbow was the result of the dancing rays of the sun.

All was quiet except for Ignoramus, the black bird. He was singing to himself and jumping from limb to limb.

Professor Hooping Crane came strolling through the woods and seeing Ignoramus he decided to stop and talk for a minute. Everyone in the forest knew that Ignoramus was a fool, including Professor Crane.

"Hello Ignoramus. How are you this fine day?" asked the Professor.

"Oh, I'm happy, very happy-happy, because I'm going to be rich, because there's a rainbow in the sky, and at the end of it there's a big pot of gold."

"Gold.  Did you say gold at the end of that rainbow?"

"Yes, yes, but you better hurry if you want any because there's only two pots, one on each end, and I have claimed one; so hurry, hurry before someone else gets there before you,"  said the black bird as he jumped up and down excitedly.

Professor Crane leaped into the air and started flying as fast as he could in the direction of the rainbow.  Seeing this, Ignoramus rolled with laughter and said, "It is better to be Ignorant, Than to be a Professor of Half Truths."

-End-

*    *    *

Your learning experience is a personal thing.  Damn the course others took, find your own way.

I'm not telling you how to learn, I'm only telling you the things you must study.  I point you in the right direction, then it's up to you to get there.

You will rise above society when you learn more, or enough, about it.

## Chapter Eleven

## IDENTITY

**IF YOU CAN'T SEE THE WORLD AS IT RELATES** to you then you have no idea as to what the world looks like.

It's the making of an identity that creates, or shapes, our eyes so that we can see the world that we live in, from our own point of views.

When we can see the world, and see ourselves in it, then we can learn society's rules and laws. Then we understand what we can and can't do. Also, having respect for the Supreme Being, we learn how to respect society's religion, or ladder to ascend to God. Anyone who ascends to God can't be all bad, right?

After learning society's limitations and spiritual aspirations, laws, and religion, there's nothing left but for you to establish your personal code.

Your personal code is the power to chain that old devil called society, and compel him to serve your every need.

I intend to deal with Knowledge of Self and Personal Code in this chapter. I will also make some general statements on life and death. But let me warn you again, that you must have your own learning experience. I can't emphasize that enough. You must search for the truth in all matters. Like Paul said, "Prove all things, and that which you find true, hold fast to it."

As you accumulate truths, a pattern of preferences, likes and dislikes will manifest themselves to you. That is the beginning of self-awareness. The values that you choose, are those which will give you purpose and a pursuit of happiness.

But what happens if you constantly accept the values that are intentionally or unintentionally imposed upon you?" I'll tell you. You wouldn't have a leg to stand on. If you were left alone in a deserted place, you would tremble in fear because there wouldn't be anyone around to tell you what to do.

That reminds me of the story of the rabbit and the squirrel.

\*　　　　　\*　　　　　\*

## THE RABBIT AND THE SQUIRREL

A rabbit and a squirrel were having a lot of fun, as they played games of tag and hide and seek. This frolic of gaiety was not at all unusual for these two fellows.

Sometimes their games would last from sun up 'till sun down.

But today something unusual happened. Just as they went tumbling through the tall grass, dashing into the underbrush, and running around the base of an old oak tree, the squirrel saw a hole in the ground, so he ducked in it with the rabbit hot in pursuit.

Before the rabbit could enter the hole, the squirrel jumped out again, and he began to shout with great excitement.

"Wow. This hole is full of nuts. I never saw so many nuts," said the squirrel, as he paused to catch his breath. Then he continued.

"Wow. There are enough nuts in there to last us for the whole Spring, Summer, and Winter. Man, we'll never run out of nuts."

Again the squirrel paused to catch his breath. But this time he noticed that the rabbit was not showing any signs of excitement. The rabbit was just sitting there wiggling his nose and stroking his ears with his paws.

"Just look at all those nuts. Man, have you ever seen so many nuts?"

The rabbit just sat there.

"Hey! What's the matter with you? Don't you realize that we're rich?" asked the squirrel.

"If you can interpret those nuts in terms of carrots for me, then maybe I too could get excited," said the rabbit.

Don't try to impose your values upon your friends.

What Is Valuable To One May Be Worthless To Another.

-End-

If I said to you, "Nixon just hit the numbers for one million dollars," it wouldn't mean a damn thing to you, now would it? You get the message?

*         *         *

## KNOWLEDGE OF SELF

What is all this talk about knowledge of self?

As far back as history will allow our research, we find wise men, prophets, and philosophers along with every other intelligent source, offering to the world the same old adage; KNOW THEY SELF.

Doesn't everyone know their own self? It seems that all you would have to do is to look in a mirror, or feel your face, or scratch your back, or know what things you like or dislike to have complete knowledge of self, so it would seem.

But if you believe that the above is all that is needed to qualify you with a knowledge of self, then you are wrong, and you need to study what follows.

Know thy self, simply means to know your destiny, or BE in this world whatever you want to be. Once a man decides what he's going to be in life, he can then say that he knows himself. He is then like a ship holding its course through the ocean of life. He doesn't change his course, whether it be stormy or fair weather, so he must reach his destination.

On the other hand, if you don't know who you are or what you want to be, your life is like a ship in very troubled waters, without a rudder (purpose) to give it direction, subject to going wherever the great waves of life take it.

Every man is created with freedom of will power.  Man is free to use that power for right or wrong.  Every man is subject to the Divine Law of Justice, which is the law of Cause and Effect which means that you must Reap What You Sow.   These great laws of nature will respond equally for the king or the beggar.  Whoever will fix his mind on being somebody, or something in life, has only to exert some effort in that direction, and the above natural laws will work for him and bring knowledge of what and how to get where he's going.

This is knowledge of self and that is the only way a man can experience true peace of mind.  That is doing what you want to do and being what you want to be.

Peace of mind is the direct result of having a personal code, or purpose in life.  As long as we are gainfully pursuing that which makes us happy, we are at peace.  Anything that takes us off our desired course, causes us discontent.

That reminds me of the story of the raccoon and the bear.

*          *          *

## THE RACCOON AND THE BEAR

A raccoon was sitting by a pond eating a fish when a bear came along.

"What a poor meal.  Why do you eat cold fish?" asked the bear.

"It is all that I can get," answered the raccoon.

"Come with me and I'll show you what a good meal is." The bear said.

So the raccoon followed the bear until they came to an old hollow log.

"Try this," said the bear as he broke open the log, sending bees flying in every direction.

The bear reached in a paw and pulled out some honey, then he and the raccoon began to eat.

The bees were alarmed and began to light upon the two intruders. The bear's thick fur protected him from being stung by the bees, but the poor raccoon was being stung from head to toe.

The bear said, "Didn't I tell you that this would be a delicious meal?"

The raccoon could stand no more, so he began to run away.

"Wait," said the bear. "Why do you run? This is a very good meal."

The raccoon was now running as fast as he could, trying to elude a swarm of bees, as he called back to the bear saying:

"It is Better to Eat Cold Fish In Contentment, Than to Eat Honey In Fear for Your Life."

-End-

The raccoon recognized that he was out of his elements, because he knew what his elements were. If he didn't, then he'd still be there trying to act like the bear, while getting stung to death.

A Personal Code is your private declaration of independence. Regardless of your station in life, you are made equal with all men; in that, you are free to pursue your goals at your own pace and design.

## PERSONAL CODE

A personal code is a system of knowledge that a person discovers for himself. He then follows this new found system in order to accomplish an end which the person considers of value. I say, to have a personal code, you must be a learned man.

Values are the basic motivation of all people, but not all people develop their own way of obtaining these values. Most of us are born in a society where our values, and the code by which we are permitted to achieve those values, is already decided for us.

It's not often that a man is born who doesn't conform to conventional values, but when this does happen, that one is called a misfit. I say, to have a personal code, your actions must show dissatisfaction with imposed values and society must label you a misfit.

Different societies treat the misfit differently. In the so-called "civilized societies," the misfit stands a very small chance of living to adulthood, without being placed in a mental or correctional institution. This is because our civilization does not recognize creative non-conformity.

Most primitive societies, and some tribes of American Indians, treated the misfit as if he was a special person. As soon as the young misfit was old enough, the elders of the tribe would take the young man away from the rest of the tribe, to an old cave or some other secluded place. Here they would leave him with food and clothing.

The misfit could not return to his tribe until he had received new revelations, through prayer, that would improve the living conditions of his tribe. That being done, the misfit is then accepted back in the tribe as a savior, witch doctor, or chief. To have a personal code, you must be an independent thinker.

Wise men of ancient times say that a misfit passes through three stages of development before he is able to create his own code. The stages are as follows: The beast of burden, the lion, and the child.

The beast of burden stage is the man who becomes dissatisfied with the rules and laws of society, so that everything about society becomes too much of a burden for him to bear. The lion stage is when the man breaks away from society's dictates, fighting violently any attempt to make him conform. The lion wins his freedom.

The child stage is when the man has won his freedom. He now emerges as an innocent being, having no associates or guidance. He is in need of direction. The child becomes a student of the world in search of knowledge. After the child accumulates knowledge, then he develops a code and progresses to a state of maturity.

After discovering where he wants to go, what he wants to do, it's then easy to create a system or code that will get him there. "Get knowledge, get wisdom, but in all your getting, get understanding."

Unless you become as little children, there is no other way out. Children are usually self-centered and have to be taught to share. So I think it's only fair to warn you to be on your guard against becoming an ego maniac, which reminds me of the story of the owl and the skunk.

*        *        *

## THE OWL AND THE SKUNK

It was a bright summer day. There was not a cloud in the clear blue sky. The forest was alive with busy bees kissing the flowers, and birds of many hues played games in the leafy trees. Such a pleasant day didn't need to be disturbed. But out of some dark hole came a skunk who was drunk from self-praise. This braggart staggered from place to place singing his self-praise song.

"Oh, how beautiful I am. Oh, how beautiful I am."

Up in a tree sat an owl nodding peacefully. The skunk looked up and noticed that the owl was not paying his royal presence any attention and yelled.

"Hey, you up there. Wake up. Listen when I'm speaking to you."

The owl shook himself, looked, and said, "Whoo?"

"You, that's who!" said the skunk in the most unpleasant ways he could muster.

"Just look at me. Ain't I the most beautiful animal in the whole world?"

"Whoo?" said the owl as he peered down at the big mouth youth.

"Me! me. That's who. I have a beautiful color. It's black with a streak of white down my smooth and sleek back. See how proud I am? Watch me walk. I'm also fearless. Every animal in the forest steps aside when they see me coming," said the skink as he pranced about beneath the tree.

The owl began to nod and the skunk could take no more of his disinterest.

"You people have no respect for true beauty. I don't know why I waste my time with your kind."

The skunk then tossed his head into the air and danced off.

The owl shook his head in dismay and said, "The Poor Fellow is so Boastful He Can't Even Sense the Odiousness of His Own Presence."

-End-

*                    *                    *

So guard yourself against becoming a stinker in the nostrils of society. Also, you must guard against becoming overly neurotic. I define the neurotic as the person who will see two birds sitting on a fence and swear that those birds are discussing him in a derogatory manner. Nervousness and fear are what cause this condition of weakness.

When you are not sure of yourself, you should never act, or you will regret it every time. That reminds me of the story of the fox and the weasel.

*                    *                    *

## JUDGE FOX AND THE WEASEL

It was peaceful and quiet near the old pond in the forest. All the inhabitants were going about their daily occupations as usual. The beavers were busy constructing a new dam. Spring had brought prosperity to the old pond community. Fathers were boasting of the new arrivals in their families. Mothers rushed here and there trying to keep their children out of trouble.

Then to everyone's surprise, a blood chilling scream broke the silence.

"Help! Help! Please somebody, help me. Someone has stolen my eggs!" cried Mrs. Ringneck Duck.

The women gathered around Mrs. Duck and tried to console her. The men glanced at each other in bewilderment.

Constable Black Bear said, "Sound the alarm. Call the council. I'll send someone to get Judge Fox."

The constable had three suspects by the time the old judge hobbled into the assembly. Leaning on his walking stick with one hand, and holding his rheumatic back with the other, he entered the gathering amid shouts of "Sock it to 'em judge. Sock it to 'em. Put 'em in the jail and throw away the key," the crowd encouraged.

Constable Bear said, "These three suspects were each seen near Mrs. Duck's house about the time her eggs were discovered missing."

Old Judge Fox looked at the three for a long time and then said, "Fatso Beaver, what were you doing near Mrs. Duck's house?"

"I was getting some sticks for the dam, and I can prove it."

"Frisky Raccoon, what were you doing?"

"I was fishing and I caught three fish. I can prove it."

The Judge fixed his gaze upon the weasel. "And you there, Sneaky the Weasel, what were you doing near Mrs. Duck's house?"

"Nothing. I was just passing by," Sneaky said, obviously nervous.

Judge Fox pointed his walking stick in the air, and he looked up, as though he was listening for someone to speak to him from above. The crowd was quiet as they watched the Judge and wondered what was happening.

"It's all clear to me now," he exclaimed. In a loud voice he said, "I see the culprit. I know his name."

"Tell us who it is. Let us know his name," The crowd shouted.

"If he doesn't confess before I reveal his identity to you, then we'll pluck his eyes out," said the Judge.

The crowd yelled, "Yes, pluck his eyes out!"

"And we'll skin him alive."

"Yes skin him alive!  Skin him alive!" the crowd repeated.

The weasel was becoming more and more nervous with every pronouncement.  Visibly shaken, he began to look for an avenue of escape, but the crowd was too thick.

The Old Fox looked at Sneaky the Weasel and said, "If he doesn't confess we'll burn him alive."

"Burn him!  Burn him!"

The weasel couldn't take it any longer, "I did it!  I stole the eggs and ate them.  Don't pluck my eyes out.  Don't burn me alive.  I confess.  I confess." cried the weasel as he fell to the feet of the Judge and begged for mercy.

"Take him to jail," commanded the Judge, as he called the trial to an end.

Black Bear the constable, scratched his head and asked, "How did you know that the weasel was guilty?"

Judge Fox smiled and said, "Where There's No Guilt, There's No Fear."

-End-

*      *      *

You always feel guilty when you do things against your better judgment.  You feel good, confident, strong, and fearless when you act in a manner that you know is right.  Right action gets you to your goal of perfection quickest.

Life is far from being easy, only the strong survive.

*       *       *

## HARD TO LIVE, EASY TO DIE

"A Winner never quits and a quitter never wins." Life has never been meant to be an easy game to play. The rules have been fixed so that the game of life gets more difficult by the decade.

The winners are judged by the amount of difficulties they have the ability and strength to surmount. The winners are given titles such as: leader, prime minister, president, king, queen, prophet and God.

Because the game of life must progressively get harder, these winners get the opportunity to lay down the ground rules for the difficulties that the future winners must overcome in the next generation.

But in all this hardness, there is mercy. Nobody has to play. If you find that life is too complicated, and you can't fit in, all you have to do is cop out.

Notice how the suicide rate keeps climbing as civilization becomes more advanced? Well that's the whole purpose of the game, to get rid of the weak ones who can't cope.

It's the easiest thing in the world to die. If you kill yourself, you have done nothing; but it is hard as hell to live and be somebody.

Can you imagine what you would be facing if you decided to be a winner? Try it you may like it.

"A winner never quits and a quitter never wins."

*     *     *

## MAKING WAVES

Think of life's processes as waves.

Do you consider yourself unique?  We come into this world through the miraculous phenomenon called birth.

We make a few waves, and vanish, only to give way to other wave makers.

Do you really think that your wave making is different?  Most people think that.  But just for a minute, think of the many waves in the oceans, seas, lakes, rivers, ponds, streams, brooks, and springs. How are your waves or ripples different?

You may say, Muhammad, Jesus, Moses, and Buddha are all different.  I say, not different, but perfect in their wave making.

Does it humble you to be told that you are just like everybody else?  If so, then you are going to be alright.

The Perfect Ones must have felt the same way, because history records their outstanding humanity.  They couldn't be proud once they discovered that they were just like everyone else.

So they stopped thinking and trying to be unique; realizing that there is no way of getting out of life's cycle of here-today-and-gone-tomorrow, they resolved to just be what they were -- Perfect Ones.

So be yourself and make your waves. But be a TIDAL WAVE so that those of us who are still ignorant of the above facts can see you and follow in your wake.

No we are not unique, in life or death. We come into the world struggling and leave the world struggling. All the while life and death sits watching, so impartial, they look bored. That brings me to my last story. It's about death.

## THE HAWK MEETS DEATH

The gray clouds frowned as the cold wind sang a mournful song and tossed the fallen leaves to and fro. The hawk was flying high in the autumn sky. So dark was the sky, you couldn't see very far, even if you had the hawk's keen eye sight.

Hungry and exhausted from flying all morning, the young hawk was about to give up the search for a meal, when he noticed a small snake slithering across an open patch of dry ground. "This is my chance," thought the hawk as he swooped down, at full speed, upon the unsuspecting serpent.

No sooner had his talons clutched the snake, than he felt a sharp sting on his leg. Discovering that he had just picked up a copperhead, he turned it loose, as he flew to a nearby tree.

"Oh, what a fool I am," said the hawk as he sat in the tree waiting for death to come.

"I should have taken a closer look before I leaped," he said to himself.

Too weak now, because the effects of the poison had begun to take effect, to hold on to the branch – he fell to the ground. Seeing death approaching, the hawk began to protest.

"Go away. Leave me alone. What have I done to you?" the hawk said, with tears in his eyes.

"Please. Please don't be angry with me. I don't know what you did, nor do I know what the master wants with you. My job is just to escort you to Him. So don't blame me, I just work here," said death as he shrugged his shoulders in an expression of indifference.

"Hush now, Mr. Hawk. Here, perch yourself on my arm. I will take you to the master and He will be glad to hear all of your protest," said Death as he and the hawk faded into the gray clouds.

Death Comes Shrugging His Shoulders.


-End-


The cycle of life and death never changes. Whether we be rich man, beggar, or thief; life and death are indifferent to us. But an alive dog is better than a dead king, so strive to make something of yourself through learning.

## Chapter Twelve

## RELIGION

**THERE'S NO GOD OUTSIDE OF MAN, AND THERE** is no man outside of God. Do you still doubt that man is God?

Today we are building homes with controlled atmospheres. Even our cars, planes, and trains have it. If we continue to pollute the air, and I don't see any end to it, we will have to build new homes under big glass bubbles with controlled atmospheres. At that time we will have to pay Public Service for air to breathe. Now, do you still think that man isn't God? Who do you think Jesus was?

We're always a little neurotic when faced with a new situation. The proper attitude for confronting a new thing is to always look for the truth of the matter. We all start off shaky, but truth gradually proves to us that

"The only thing to fear is fear itself." But how many of us are lucky enough to learn just that simple truth in a life time?

Why is truth so scarce that it takes some people 35 and even 50 years before they can accumulate enough of it to excel in our societies? What has caused such a drought to befall on mankind?

Religion is the cause and I will explain how. But first let me remind you that we shouldn't be prejudiced in our search for knowledge. We should keep an open mind and accept the truth from wherever it can be found.

We should be like the honey bee, who searches for nectar and is only concerned with whether a flower has some or not. He doesn't care about the size or color of the flower or its location. The bee is successful because he attunes himself to accept nectar wherever he finds it. Think of how limited the bee would be if he only accepted nectar from tulips.

Truth is our basic nature, we seek it in all that we do. We have a built-in mechanism which is attuned to truth, so any time we read or hear truth something inside us says, "That's right." So whether you like what I am about to say concerning the church and the preachers or not, is not the point. You will know if it is the truth and it will be left up to you to panic or be cool.

The search for truth is the greatest good, and the Originator of Truth is God. Knowledge of truth is power. No man comes to power by what he has in his pockets, because a fool and his money are soon parted. It's what he has in his head that makes him powerful. So without any further delay, I now give you my understanding of religion.

The scarcity of truth in the world today is due to religion. All clergy are the same, regardless of their calling. Religion represents the ladder or a set of steps, by which its adherents can ascend to God, or a God-like state. That's the true purpose of all religions. But due to thousands of years of corruption, the true purpose of the church, mosque, and temple were lost to the masses, except for a few.

The trouble started when the Prophets, Buddhas, and Gods passed the Divine Revelation down to the clergymen. Our clergy are no different from you or I. They're from amongst us, and are subject to the same Divine Laws as we are. We always make the mistake of thinking that they're different. When God says, "The devil will tempt you," we automatically think that doesn't apply to the clergy; but the devil even tried to Tempt God. So the clergy are far from being an exception to falling for evil suggestions.

When the prophets brought new truths, the clergy would cleverly pick out the choice pieces and keep that for themselves. Needless to say, those stolen pieces turned out to be the keys to the proper understanding of the Divine Revelations.

If we tried to ascend to heaven on the strength of the sermons they preach to us, we would never make it. Even if we had the best equipped moonship on Cape Canaveral, we still couldn't get off the ground without the ignition keys.

Sure, some of you will sympathize with the clergy because in a sense they are right. A little knowledge sometimes is a very dangerous thing. Wisdom placed in the hands of fools is like putting a five year old in a lethal jet fighter. Yes, we would abuse the power of truth like we do our parks, rivers, and neighborhoods. But what was considered carefulness in the beginning on the part of the clergy hiding the truth, turned out to be pure greed in the end.

They kept these important keys from us; wouldn't allow any of it to be written in books, passing it on only by word of mouth. This insured the secrets of the keys. The trouble with that plan was that when death came to a clergy, if he didn't reveal all he knew before he died, then he took many of the secret keys with him.

One of the first and most important truths they concealed was true identity of God. This was done by telling the people God was a spirit and not a man. They knew that if they taught the masses that God is a man, they would soon have no need of the church, mosque or temple, nor would we need the clergy to show us the way to find God.

So the devil, who is also a man, enticed the clergy to keep special parts of the truth secret, assuring them that the masses would then be their willing slaves. From that time on the clergy became more and more corrupt, and Divine knowledge became more and more of a secret.

The world is divided between two kinds of people, those who know, and those who don't. That reminds me of the wise uncle and his two nephews.

A wise uncle and his two nephews were on their way to the temple when they passed an old Buddhist monk sitting by the road side, lolling his head back and forth, and making strange sounds. The uncle said to his two nephews, "Which of you can give me an unrefutable answer as to the condition of that old monk we passed just now?" Then he added, "I will give the one with the correct answer some sweet meat."

"He is sick," said the first of the two.

"He is in the spirit of his faith," said the second.

The uncle then gave the sweet meats to the one who said the monk was in the spirit. The other nephew said, "But wasn't I right also?"

"Yes," said the uncle. "But in making that statement you have left yourself open to attack. If we know where you stand on a subject, then we can challenge you anytime we want. You're right to assume that the old monk was sick, due to the fact that we accept what everyone does in common to be normal, and the person who acts in any other way, we say they're sick or crazy. But you must understand that when you tell the public the truth about where you stand, or what you understand, that truth is what they will use to condemn you. Because all Gods of the past were condemned because of the very truth they revealed to the people. You, my nephew, will have to struggle through life as all truthful men before you."

"On the other hand, your brother will be rich and famous, and he will live a long and easy life. His answer was that the monk was in the spirit. This makes him safe from reproach. No one knows what he means by that, so they can't say he's wrong, and your brother knows that his argument is fool-proof, because the public will never catch up with that spirit to make it tell whether he lied or not. So, already he is to be rewarded for his genius."

"You should strive hard to get knowledge, because that is the only thing that man can ever possess. Knowledge is the only thing between man and the pit. You survive as long as you have the ability to avoid a downfall. No man can survive for another."

That reminds me of the story of the two Tibetan brothers who were sent to the monastery to be educated. At the conclusion of their studies they were to meet God face to face.

One brother was very studious and bright. The other was lazy and never did his homework. When tests were given the lazy one copied the answers of his smart brother. Graduation came and the high priest instructed the lazy brother to go in the garden of the monastery, and there he would find God waiting for him.

The lazy one ran to the garden, but all he say was an old man plowing a furrow in the garden, He said to himself, "God had hidden Himself from me because He knows I'm not really qualified to meet Him." Full of guilt, he left the monastery with a broken heart.

The high priest then told the smart brother to go to the garden, and that there he would find God. The smart one went to the garden, and seeing the old man at the plow, he bowed deep and said, "Greetings my Lord. I am your humble servant. I have been sent to you by the high priest and I pray you find me acceptable."

The old man smiled and made a deep bow. Then he said, "Yes, I have been waiting for you. I've just finished plowing so let's go over there in the shade. I have a pot of tea and butter. We can sit and talk."

After they were seated the old man passed a cup of tea and said, "Your brother couldn't see past the veil of ignorance, so he passed on into the world of darkness. I know how you tried to help him, but no one can see or know for another. But now my Lord, let's talk about you and the work you're destined to perform."

The smart one was shocked, and he asked, "Why do you refer to me, your servant, as your Lord?"

"Because you became a God the moment you stepped through the veil of ignorance—into the world of eternal light."

"When did I step through the veil?"

"The moment that you recognized that I was God, not a peasant. Only a God can recognize God in another man."

This is just part of an ancient story revealing two keys: How to rule the masses, and the knowledge of God being a man; these can only be discovered through knowledge.

Look around you. There are secret orders of everything. The mystic orders, the Masons the Christian Knights, the Elks, and would you believe the secret order of the bull moose. There are thousands of secret orders and all of them represent another ring of missing keys.

The prophets always gave up all the truths because they understood that truth is divinely protected. But those entrusted to pass it on are the ones who would give up little and hide much.

A devil can't cross over to heaven, but an angel can move freely between both worlds. Everything in heaven and hell seeks to destroy the devil; but everything in both worlds only serve to strengthen the angel.

Without the keys, the above statement is very confusing. Especially when we add that to the fact that most of us still think of heaven as up above, and hell as something down below. That's nothing but modern day superstition. Heaven and hell are conditions of the mind, not places that we go to. If understood properly, the heaven above is only to indicate a high office, or high authority; also height of wisdom and understanding. Below is to indicate the low and debasement of fallen humanity. The fire and hell is mass emotional insecurity and self-degradation. This is the fabled mourning of hells inhabitants.

A thin mental veil separates the wise and the contented angelic being from the ignorant, pessimistic complaining of an evil person. Example: Two men sitting on a public bus, one is cheerful-the world is a beautiful place to him. The man next to him wishes he had an atomic bomb so that he could kill every bastard on the planet. Heaven and hell are both in the mind, not places that we go to.

Nothing is good or bad until man gets his hands on it. Good or righteousness, bad or evil, are forces of energy. Like positive and negative. You can't be wise unless you know your ignorance. If you can channel these forces of positive and negative, and make them work together for you, then you can become so powerful that your knowledge would light up a whole city; like Ben Franklin and his electricity. Today a city, tomorrow the world.

As long as you fail to understand the workings of good and evil, you will not progress far. Try to light an electric lamp with just one cord and nothing will happen. It takes the positive and the negative. Again, you can't be wise unless you know your ignorance. You can't be righteous unless you know your evils. If I know that I'm wrong, I know how to get right. That understanding makes a virtue of sin.

If the preachers and the clergymen would have taught you these things, truth would be flowing so abundantly, we would again be diocesans of the deep. But the preachers and clergy were more worried about their treasury than they were of saving souls. You are left starving for truth and praying for another prophet to come. You'll think twice before you let anyone kill the next one, won't you?

God Is. There is always one man on your planet who is wiser than all of us put together. He's the Supreme Being.

He's distinguished by His ability to transform the lives of all those who come in contact with Him. An ignorant man becomes wise in His presence. The sick get well and the blind see. There has never been a time when such a man was not in existence. Gods come and go like any other man, but there's never a time when a Supreme One is not on this planet.

The Bible is a book of revolutions. God is the only Dictator who informs a civilization, thousands of years ahead of time, that He will overthrow its government; and He performs a successful take-over every time. That's to prove to you that God isn't dead; that God is very much alive and planning another overthrow. This one will be the biggest one yet.

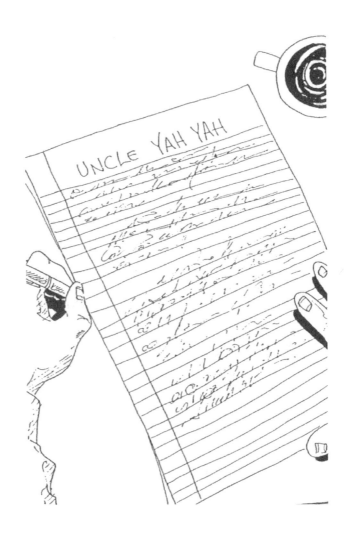

## Chapter Thirteen

### WISDOM

### FROM THE LIPS OF UNCLE YAH YAH

Your evil is the measure of your good.

\*　　\*　　\*

They say the blind and the seeing are not alike. I say they are, in that both can't tell the other what he sees.

\*　　\*　　\*

Man can't rise any higher than his lowest desire.

\*　　\*　　\*

Fame has always been two faced, exalting and debasing at the same time.

We despair only to give expression to our greater hopes.

* * *

I have only learned that I have yet to learn.

* * *

To defend yourself is good, but to be unoffendable is better.

* * *

Your afflictions are self-imposed, so if you accept credit for your success, then accept blame for your failures too.

* * *

The day that God raises a family, drives an automobile, flies in a jet plane, watches television, and reads a news-paper then that's the Day of Judgment.

* * *

Sometimes silence speaks the loudest.

* * *

The pursuit of God, and the pursuit of pleasure, have been a major conflict with man for ages. Why doesn't he pursue his pleasure through God, or pursue God through his pleasures? That would, at least, resolve the conflict.

* * *

Disaster is like a storm, here today and gone tomorrow. The ability to survive such a calamity depends on whether you are proud and stubborn, like the tall oak tree, or humble and yielding like the palm tree. A storm comes and the oak is torn up by the roots; but the palm tree bends with the wind and stand straight again-as if nothing had happened.

*   *   *

If God can't stand to hear my complaints, then He is not worthy of my praise.

*   *   *

You may call me a saint, but you will have to ignore my evil deeds. You may call me a devil, but you will have to ignore my righteousness. So regardless of what you call me, your ignorance of me is unavoidable.

*   *   *

Tend to your own store, or mind your business; its meaning doesn't change no matter how you say it.

*   *   *

Learning to speak well, is difficult, but learning when not to speak is harder.

*   *   *

Your mouth is the instrument by which you are exalted or condemned.

*   *   *

Man is like a tree, the more he aspires to the heights and lights, the more strongly his roots strive earthwards into the darkness and deep into evil.

*   *   *

"I'm doing what you let me do, Lord," is the prayer of pious man, though he be drunk when he says it.

\* \* \*

There would be no ugly women, if there weren't any ugly men.

\* \* \*

Civilization is like the moon, advancing by degrees to fullness; then declining in the same manner to its end.

\* \* \*

The greater the light the less man sees.

\* \* \*

What is original, the thing made or the thing thought of?

\* \* \*

What would a man love if you took his dream?

\* \* \*

A man who loses control when excited is like a man who drinks to forget. After he is sober from his drunkenness, or excitement, the situation is still the same.

\* \* \*

Life is like a motorized pendulum on a clock, the motor is desire; you will not stop going to the extreme until the motor (desire) stops running.

\* \* \*

The greater the acceptance of a person's good, the greater the acceptance of his faults.

It is that which is said that makes civilization rise or fall.

*   *   *

Truth is that which is, time evolves from the truth; time is motion, truth stands still.

*   *   *

There are as many ways to see a thing as there are people to see it.

*   *   *

People accept that which is current so as not to be thought of as ignorant; but as soon as it passes, they laugh at how ignorant they used to think and act.

*   *   *

To have complete power over others, you must become a slave to the principles that promise to entrust you with such an ability.

*   *   *

No pleasure is lost, it goes to make way for a better pleasure.

*   *   *

You must first learn of your uncertainty before you can ever begin to be certain.

*   *   *

There could be no concept of what far is, if it was not for those who go to the extreme.

*   *   *

Little mistakes give birth to big improvements.

What would a smooth road be if we didn't have a bumpy one to compare it with?

*     *     *

Man has not fulfilled himself, so he's in a state of continuous dissatisfaction. He will not rest until he is God.

*     *     *

It is their respect that begets their contempt.

*     *     *

It is by our own hands that we are tortured the most.

*     *     *

Your great display of virtue is vanity; throw them both into the garbage can.

*     *     *

Your greatest enemy is you.

*     *     *

Don't be greedy and nothing will swallow you up.

*     *     *

If you judge me you lay down the rules for your own judgment.

*     *     *

There is no such thing as a good or bad day, it all depends on the way you feel.

*     *     *

There is a positive and a negative side of every situation, but we always look at one side, and then regret our shortsightedness.

The mind of man is separated into three parts; self-consciousness of what he wants to do; consciousness of what society wants him to do; and consciousness of what God wants him to do.  No wonder the world is full of confusion.

## Chapter Fourteen

## THE TRANSFORMATION

**I SPENT ALL OF SUNDAY AFTERNOON** reading Uncle Yah Yah's manuscript, and it was just like he said, all that I needed to know was right there. There were three chapters that were made up of short stories, essays, and wise sayings. I just couldn't put it down until I had finished every page. It was a unique learning experience for me and I wondered how so much wisdom could be contained in such a small manuscript. I almost couldn't believe my eyes. Every time I put it down, I'd be compelled to pick it up again. I read certain parts two and three times, and was still totally involved when Freda came to see me.

"Is anybody home? Hey in there, is anybody home?"

"Yes, I'm sorry I didn't hear you. I was reading Uncle Yah Yah's manuscript. Come on in, the door's open."

"Well how do you like it?" she asked, closing the door behind her.

"I'm about to bust with excitement. This thing is really great. I'm glad you came by because I just have to talk with someone about this. Sit down and make yourself comfortable."

"Didn't I tell you that Uncle Yah Yah was something else?" she said, as she sat down on the side of the bed.

"Yes, and you were right. You should read some of the stuff he says in this manuscript."

"I have, and I knew you'd like it."

"Freda, everything Uncle Yah Yah says here is nothing but the plain truth. It's just as he said, "We're all little people caught up in the machinery of society. We're processed and numbered like any other manufactured article. We have no life of our own. What do most of us know about a pursuit of happiness? Where would we find the time to pursue anything but a raise in pay? Only the super rich are free, and they make their own rules or standards to live by and they pay society's cattlemen to keep us, the masses, in line. It's really something to discover that you're a puppet. It's kind of frightening, but somehow I'm glad to be facing up to it for the first time in my life. As a matter of fact, after reading what Uncle Yah Yah has to say, I feel my whole attitude towards society and religion is changing. Do you know what I'm trying to say Freda?"

"Yes, I think I can sum it up by saying, the

beginning of knowledge starts with the discovery of your ignorance. Uncle Yah Yah said that you will be alright once you start examining yourself."

"Uncle Yah Yah said that?"

"Yes, and he knew you were angry because he cut your interview short."

"Yeah, why did he do that Freda, do you know?"

"He said that you appeared to him like a leopard. His reason for saying that is because the leopard doesn't just kill for food, he kills for pleasure and his prey is usually smaller than himself. Uncle Yah Yah said your character is like that. You're very mean to people you believe to be in a lower station in life than you. But like I told you, he thinks you'll be alright when you can see yourself."

"I've been called many things before, but never a leopard. I'll have to look into that."

"I'm sure you'll agree with him after you've thought about it."

"How does a person become a member of Uncle Yah Yah's organization, Freda?"

"Truth is our only bond, there's nothing to join."

"Well who teaches the doctrine to the masses?"

"Those who believe that Uncle Yah Yah's telling the truth, take it upon themselves to teach it. That's all. Uncle Yah Yah says that if they believe it they will automatically preach it. It's as simple as that."

"Freda, I'm so excited over this manuscript. Why,

I've forgotten to ask you what it was you wanted to see me about."

She smiled and crossed her big pretty legs and said, "Well you told me when you first met me that if ever I felt charitable to let you know, so here I am feeling very charitable."

I couldn't believe my ears. I didn't know what to do or say. My hands and forehead began to sweat. I felt like I was about to faint when the old Don Juan in me took control of the situation. As cool as an Eskimo puppy, I leaned forward and placed my hand on her knee, and rubbing it very gently. I said, "That's very good Freda, and I'm going to do my best to make you happy you came here tonight. I was going to leave this evening, but now that you're here, nothing could move me til morning."

While she prepared the bed, I called home to let them know I wouldn't be back until Monday morning. When I got back to the cabin, Freda had taken off everything but her slip. I undressed ceremoniously, folding and hanging up my clothes, confident that if there was an award for sexual performance, then I was going to win first place that night.

I cut the light out, got in bed, and pulled her to me. Our lips met and time stood still. Whether we made love for five minutes or five hours, I don't know. I can only remember her silky smooth nakedness, and our limbs struggling as we tied ourselves in a human knot. I felt the rhythm of reciprocal motion, and the wildness of it produced a most heavenly serenity. Limp as two rag dolls, we layed as I kissed her happy tears.

Monday morning I said my goodbyes with as little formality as possible, then left. I felt like an angel leaving heaven.

Now what kind of angel would I make, I thought, and had to laugh at my poor self-reflection. But on second thought, if Uncle Yah Yah's right when he says, "Everyman is as good as he is evil," then I might make a pretty good angel at that. Yeah, Uncle Yah Yah had given me second thoughts about a lot of things.

Like what he said about me being like a leopard. It's true that my attitude has always been black middle-class and snobbish. I considered only professional people my equal. What a fool I must look like walking around with a better-than-thou air. I thought of the many people I'd mauled with insults, simply because I considered them to be lesser station than myself. Like that young girl at the Top Hat Club I'd embarrassed when I stopped there for a drink on my way up here. Just thinking about that scene made me feel rotten inside.

I noticed that I wasn't far from the Top Hat Club, so I decided to stop and see if I could find her. She said her name was Elly, or Elsie. It was something like that. Anyway, I knew I'd recognize her if I saw her again. The Club couldn't have been more than a few minutes away.

Meanwhile, my thoughts turned to Freda, and a warm feeling passed over me. She was really something else. She was meek but you could feel the strength of her character. She was a totally free spirit. Yeah, that's it. She isn't under the yoke of society, she's above it.

Lost in thought, I almost passed the TOP HAT. I pulled into the empty parking lot and went into the club. The place was almost deserted. Only the bartender was at the bar. I didn't feel like a drink, and was too ashamed to ask the bartender if he'd seen a girl whose name I wasn't sure of, and stood about so tall, and looked like this and that. Deciding that it would be an embarrassing way to describe her, I decided to leave. As I started for the door I saw her. She was trying to sneak out before I would recognize her.

"Hey Elly, wait a minute. I want to talk to you."

"My name's not Elly, its Elsie, and I'm just leaving."

She looked like a baby doll. She was a very pretty girl, and I wished I could help her in some way. She was too young and pretty to be wasting away in a place like the Top Hat.

"I'm leaving too," I said. "I stopped by just to see you. I wanted to apologize for my behavior the other day," I managed to say as we walked out towards that parking lot.

"Oh, that's alright, I'm used to things like that. In my line of business, worse than that can happen."

The thought of this beautiful girl being mistreated on a regular basis, disturbed me. I felt like picking her up, putting her in my car, and taking her home with me. I don't know what came over me, but before I could check myself, I asked that age old stupid question.

"Elsie, what's a nice girl like you doing in a place like this?"

She looked at me, her eyes were filled with emptiness as she said, "It's a long story and you wouldn't believe me if I told you. You'd probably laugh at me."

"I don't think this is a laughing matter Elsie, and I

wouldn't have asked if I wasn't concerned why you're doing what you're doing."

"Okay I'll tell you. I came from a family with a long line of prostitutes, going back for generations. My mother started teaching me the tricks of the trade when I was eight years old. My virginity was sold for $200, when I was eleven. After that, I took regular customers, but my mother kept the money I made--except for a few dollars she'd let me keep for spending money. So when I turned fourteen, I ran away with a John on his way to New York."

"My mother told me that all the women in our lineage were destined to become prostitutes because my great great grandmother sold her soul to the devil. So I don't know how to do anything else, and if I did try to do something else, I couldn't."

"You mean because of the spell that was put on your fore-parents?"

"Yes."

"How old are you now Elsie?"

"Seventeen," she softly said.

She looked more like 15 or 16. I felt sorry for her. So young and pretty, and yet so ignorant and superstitious. I wondered how many more dark beliefs and old wives tales she had clouding her young mind. How much better off she would be if only she knew that she is God or the devil at her own choosing.

If she only knew that she was not destined to follow in her mother's footsteps. I felt great pity for this poor girl. I reached in my pocket and pulled out a $20.00 bill, and placed it in her hand, I said, "Here, take this!"

"What's this for?"

"Just because you're a very pretty girl, so keep it, O.K.?"

She thanked me, as I turned to go, I said, "You take care of yourself, and who knows, we may meet again sometime."

"Okay, you too," she said as she waved and I climbed in my car.

How could she say that's all she could do, I thought to myself as I started back on the road towards home. There were thousands of things she could do. As young as she was, she had a whole lifetime ahead of her. There were many agencies and schools that would help her become whatever she wanted to be. There was vocational and on the job training.....then like a bucket of ice water being tossed in my face, it dawned on me. Why didn't I tell her that?

Telling it to myself wasn't going to help her any. I was being as bad, if not worse, than the clergy and preachers of Uncle Yah Yah's manuscript. Hiding the truth, or keeping it to myself, when it could save the life of some poor person in need. I could've told her she was just being superstitious, but I just stood there and said nothing.

Right then I promised myself, that from that time on, I would never fail to tell or write the truth, that I would teach it to the best of my knowledge whenever the occasion would arrive. That resignation made me feel good, and I thought about Freda. I remember her saying, "Those who believe the truth preach it. It's as simple as that."

Unknowingly, I had let my foot get a little heavy on the gas pedal, and by the time I noticed that I was twenty miles over the speed limit, it was already too late. The blinking lights of the State Trooper's car was signaling me to stop. I was getting my license and registration together when the Trooper said, "So we meet again, Mr. Hawkins. You're the reporter, right?"

"Yes," I said, surprised to see him again, "and believe me I'm glad to see you, even though you caught me red handed speeding. I wanted to beg your pardon for giving you a hard time the other day. I've matured enough in the last few days to realize that man must live and let live. We're all trying to survive, and when enough of us can put this attitude into practice, this world will be a heaven on earth. I hope you will accept my apology."

The trooper was writing the ticket as he listened to me. Then he stopped writing, and looked me square in the face, as if to measure my sincerity. He then closed the ticket book and put his pen back in his pocket. He said, "The other day you acted like a gangster and now you sound like a preacher. Stay within the speed limit, O.K.?" he said as he went back to his car.

I drove onto the road in a daze. I was astonished by the trooper's words. He said I sounded like a preacher. I was just thinking about that and he came right out and said I sounded like a preacher.

I stopped at the office just long enough to deliver the manuscript, and took the rest of the day off. I had some very serious thinking to do.

Tuesday morning, I walked into the boss's office and announced that I was ready to take my two weeks vacation.

"Rudy, Uncle Yah Yah's manuscript is beautiful. I've never read anything so full of wisdom in my life. So don't worry about it. We'll take care of everything from this point on," Jonathan said as he shook my hand.

"Yeah, I felt the same way about it," I said.

"You don't look too well Rudy, what's the matter?" Carol asked.

"Everything is alright, I've just got to get away for awhile, that's all."

"You finally decided to take the family to Florida. When do you want to leave?" Jonathan asked.

"No, not Florida. I have a more important place to take them, "I said, as I started out of the office. "I'll stop in a little later to work out the details of the vacation."

Down the hall from the office I stopped at the water cooler for a drink. As I bent down to fill my cup, a picture of Uncle Yah Yah came to my mind. It was as clear as if he was standing right in front of me. Then he said, "When you get away from work for awhile, come and visit me again."

## EPILOGUE

The knowledge, wisdom and understanding of self, society and religion, are the magical potions which transforms your world from a sphere of meaningless conglomerations of people, places and things and changes them into specific categories of elements to be assimilated for strength, or to be opposed for protection.

Such a character possessed of the golden elixir is referred to as Omnipresent, or living in-tune with what's happening now.

I know, because I crawled into this prison cell-like cocoon a lowly caterpillar, but I shall emerge a butterfly, dancing about and kissing the pretty flowers in the springtime of my youth. Watch for me.

-*Al Dickens*

# Order Form

## Uncle Yah Yah - 21st Century Man of Wisdom

## Part One

Please send me  _____ copy(s) of **Uncle Yah Yah – 21st Century Man of Wisdom Part One** @ $14.95 each.  Plus 6% sales tax.

Enclosed is $18.79 for one book ($14.95 + Tax $.89 + S/H $2.95). Each additional book is $15.84 ($14.95 + Tax $.89) plus $1.00 Shipping/Handling for each additional book.

### Please ship the above copy(s) to:

Name  _____

Address  _____

City, State, Zip  _____

### Please Send Check or Money Order To:

**Yah Yah & Company**
**P. O. Box 55133**
**Trenton, NJ 08638**

### Please allow 4-6 weeks for delivery!

## Uncle Yah Yah - 21st Century Man of Wisdom

## Part Two

## Available Winter 2005

ABOUT THE AUTHOR:

     Al Dickens was born in Winter Haven, Florida, March 31, 1938. He and his family (mother, father and sister) moved to Newark, New Jersey in the early forties.

     Raised in the streets of Newark's $2^{nd}$ and $3^{rd}$ wards made it almost inevitable that Al would start having serious trouble with the law by the age of 14.

     Al spent the last 16 years of his life behind prison bars as a result of two armed robbery convictions. But the prison turned out to be a golden opportunity for Al to get a formal education; and he took full advantage of it.

     By the time Al completed two years of college he had co-authored three books and was working on *Uncle Yah Yah*.

     Presently Al Dickens, has been in prison for 43 years for 18 bank robberies. He served 25 years for the state of New Jersey, and has completed 18 years in the federal prison. He will be released August 2010.